Not What You Expected

Richard Paul Mroz

PublishAmerica
Baltimore

Hardcover 978-1-4560-0062-2
Softcover 978-1-4560-0063-9
PUBLISHED BY PUBLISHAMERICA, LLLP
www.publishamerica.com
Baltimore

Printed in the United States of America

Not What You Expected

Richard Paul Mroz

Chapter 1

"Mama, Mama, come quickly, Rolando is on the roof."
The shrill voice of five year old Francesca blurted out to the
large woman at the sink who was cleaning the chicken for
dinner.

"What?" The woman turned to see who the intruder
was.

"He's on the roof," Francesca repeated pointing to the
ceiling of the basement where the Italian family did most
of their living.

Rosalina took a deep breath, put the bird into the sink,
and wiped her hands on a cloth that passed for an apron.
"You better not be lying to..."

"No, no. He's on the roof next to the chimney, really."
Francesca did not wait for a response as she turned and
charged out of the room and up the stairs to the outside.

Mama followed but at a slower pace still wiping her
hands. She thought, 'It wasn't good to stop plucking a
chicken.' Outside, she was greeted by the rest of her eight
children all pointing and screaming about Rolando. She

turned to see her brother Sal, dressed in baggy pants, coming to see what all the noise was about. It was at that time that Mama saw her small son looking into the chimney. "Rolando," Mama's voice boomed out. "What are you doing on the roof?"

"It's a bird, Mama. It got caught in the chimney and I wanted to free it," came the frail reply.

Mama looked at her children then at the sky. "Why did I have to give birth to Francis of Assisi, perche? eh?" She then turned to Rolando. "Come down, now. The bird has wings and you don't."

Just as Rolando was turning from the chimney, the bird bolted from the structure jolting the young boy who then lost his balance and his grip on the chimney. He fell to his rear, slid down the roof catching his feet on the rainspout which threw him forward into the air. The kids, Mama and Uncle Sal watched in horror as the small body catapulted into the air. No one made a sound because of fear and surprise. Uncle Sal, usually a slow moving man of peasant stock, moved adroitly to intercept Rolando. The impact sent both of them to the grass.

Only the briefest of moments existed between that impact and the cheers of the children. Rolando stared into his uncle's face, which at first had a grimace, then a smile. "Are you alright, Rolando?" he asked.

Rolando thought a moment. "Ah, yes. That was a good catch," Rolando said rolling off his uncle. "Are you okay?"

Mama came up behind Rolando before Sal could reply and lifted the boy to his feet. "You could have killed yourself. Thank God, Uncle Sal was here. Would I have caught you? No, and serves you right. If you break both of your legs don't come running to me, eh?" Once again she looked up at the sky. "Why me?" She looked at Rolando who stared up at her with innocence. "Jesus had his angels, and you have Uncle Sal."

She was about to say more in the form of some punishment, when Sal spoke. "Let me talk to him, Rosalina, then you can put him in the basement upside down with the rats." The last word came out explosively making everyone jump.

Mama looked at the other children who were all waiting to hear the Ex Cathedra requirements for the remission of sins. "What? You have nothing to do? Believe me, I can find plenty to do for all of you." The kids darted in all directions. "Except you, Maria. No, no, vienne qui. Come here."

Maria knew she had been too slow to react. "What, Mama?"

"Come with me, I need your help in the kitchen."

"But Mama..."

"No. Come. I need you in the kitchen." Mama waved her back.

Josephine, the younger girl, at seven, stopped on her escape and turned around. "Oh, Mama, I'll help in the kitchen. Let Maria go with the others. I want to help."

Mama looked at Josephine, her eyes softening to the appeal. "Okay, then come. I want you to stuff the cannolis with the special sweet ricotta and you can sample all you want." She turned her attention to Maria who was not only older by five years, but also much heavier. "Go ahead, Maria, go play, but tomorrow, there's a bathroom upstairs that needs your attention. Go. Go." Maria suddenly had second thoughts about objecting. As a matter of fact, all she could think about was that delicious cream and Josephine getting it all.

Rolando stood beside his fallen uncle staring down at the large figure. He knew that his uncle had saved him from a lot of pain and was about to thank him when his uncle, raising himself to his elbows said, "Why did you want to help that bird, Rolando?"

The boy sat next to his uncle. "Well, Uncle Sal, I thought that if an animal was in pain and we could help, we should." He studied his uncle for a reaction. "Isn't that right?"

"It's a good thought, Rolando. It's a very good thought." Sal smiled. "But now I'm in pain. Can you do anything or are your ideas just for the animals?"

Rolando thought a moment. "Ah, yes, there is that yellow stuff Mama puts on the cuts. Are you cut?"

Sal showed him a scrape on his elbow. "Does that count as a cut?" Rolando nodded when he saw some blood and ran off to get not only iodine, but a bandage and a glass of water because Mama always gave him water.

As Rolando put on the iodine getting a wince from his uncle and applied the bandage, Sal sipped some water. It was then that Yolanda the oldest girl at seventeen approached them. She sat on the grass at a distance and watched. Yolanda was cautious about everything. She played life safely. Sal looked over at her. "So, Yolanda, what have we learned?"

Yolanda moved closer in a thoughtful manner thinking how her uncle had felt the pain of the iodine more than he had felt the fall. "I suppose that you have to take a risk if you really want something and there could be pain. I suppose you can endure pain if there is a good reason." She raised her voice at the end of the statement as if questioning her answer.

"And," Sal looked at both the children, "what about pain and no cure, eh? Just pain?"

Rolando looked confused. It was a question he would face at another time, when he was older. Yolanda squinted, then said, "That's plain stupid and cruel."

Sal knew she was thinking of Stephano with whom she had had a brief but rough relationship. He stood brushing himself. "It's worse than that, Yolanda. Pain, without purpose is misery itself, but 'stupid' will do for now."

Chapter 2

As Sal returned to his work in the garden, he looked around for Antonio and Roberto to help, but as usual Antonio was probably in the woods making a tree house, laying a trap, or maybe tracking an animal. Antonio was only two years older at fourteen than Roberto but he was the leader in the woods. In school work, Roberto was the leader.

Sal stopped at the edge of the garden looking at first toward the woods, then the beehives, then the chicken coop, and even as far as the large doll house that the girls liked to play in. There was silence. Even the trees were silent and silence meant something was wrong in a house full of children.

"Antonio," Sal yelled out. "Roberto, where are you?" He waited for a response. Earlier he had heard some activity near the woods, but now there was only silence. Sal looked at his garden remembering the one he had left behind in Sicily. There in that sunny land, the soil and climate allowed him to grow grapes, olives, figs, lemons, pomadori tomatoes and the best blood oranges. There in Sicily was his heart, but there was also poverty. He sat on the large wooden barrel of water he filled every day for drinking when he got too hot.

Still listening, he slowly stood, opened the top of the barrel, dipped the copper ladle that hung on the side and he drank. The water was almost as cool as when he had filled it that morning from the spring that also fed his garden that was interlaced with small ditches and dams.

Refreshed, he picked up the hoe and as he began weeding, with the sun baking his sweat to his shirt, he remembered when his sister, Rosalina, had come to America with her husband Giorgio. That was eighteen years ago. Things went very well for them. Giorgio became a barber and taught music while Rosalina saved on the budget by tending the garden and chickens. Rosalina wanted Mama and Papa to come and although Mama was interested, Papa said he wanted to die in his own country because he was very proud of the fact that his ancestors had fought under Garibaldi to free Sicily. They convinced Sal to come and that was four years ago. The next year, little Sam came into the world, and Giorgio left it as he crossed the street not paying attention to the Paca Street trolley.

Thinking of Giorgio's death made Sal think of his wife, Donna, and his two children, Francis and Paolo. He thought of their deaths in the earthquake, six years ago, crushed under the house he had built. Sal had heard the dog, Petrarch, moaning late at night and when he went out to see the reason, a three second shake of the earth brought an end to all his hopes. Petrarch was only trying to warn them. He lifted his eyes to see his dog, Tino, lying in the sun, and his heart saddened at the memories. The buzzing of a bee brought him from the past in Cefalu, Sicily, to his present garden and the need to tend it.

'Bees?' Sal thought, looking around. 'Why should there be bees now? This is not their busy time. Have they been disturbed?' Another bee hummed near him. The hives were located at the far corner of the property just before the woods. Between him and the hives lay a fallow piece of land that had yielded an excellent crop of chick peas, zucchini, squash, favas, and asparagus. Good protein but a lot of gas. He did not need to go far to see that one of the hives had been knocked over.

He stopped and glanced about, thinking that there were no bears in the area and that a small creature could not have done the damage. He had a garden to weed and now this. Where were Antonio and Roberto? It would be nice to have another man to help with the chores, but who would marry a widow with eight children and they couldn't afford to hire someone. No, it was his job to solve the problem. He examined the fallen hive realizing that he would be stung many times before the job was done, but it needed to be done, and it had to be done alone.

With a struggle that brought streams of sweat and eight stings, Sal got the hive in place. It was then he noticed tracks in the dirt as if someone had dragged something large into the woods toward the creek.

Sal looked at the tracks then in the direction of his unweeded garden. He decided to follow the tracks that went through the woods in a fairly straight line to the creek. While under the shade of the trees he kept wondering as to the object being dragged. His curiosity was quickly and horribly satisfied when he saw the twins Maria and Roberto, and Antonio on a raft in the middle of the creek. The creek, known by the locals as Snake Pit, was not large, but it was deep. The three kids were huddled on a six by six raft without a paddle. That was bad, but what was worse was that the tide was rapidly going out. Sal began running along the shore yelling.

"Hey, Antonio, Roberto. Come in, now. The tide will take you to the bay."

"What?" came a faint reply.

"Come in, now."

"We lost our paddle."

"Uncle Sal." This time it was Maria. "Help us."

"Oh, mio Dio." Sal called to the heavens as he ran to a small beach. "Antonio, Roberto, listen to me. Take off your clothes, tie them in a line and throw it to me. Hurry, presto, capise, eh?"

"Si, Uncle Sal," replied Antonio as the two boys disrobed watching their uncle wade into the water.

The bottom was muddy and probably the home of crabs, but Sal kept walking clenching his teeth as he watched the boys quickly tie their clothes together. "Hurry, throw it to me," Sal called out. The line of clothes missed as Sal lunged forward plunging up to his neck. "Santo Diablo, try again."

This time Maria removed her clothes to add them to the boys'. Roberto and Antonio stared at their sister who turned her back to them.

"Roberto," Sal yelled. "This is not the time to look at your sister. Throw the line."

The raft was slowly gliding past the point of no return when Roberto gave a toss that reached Sal but no one had remembered to hold the other end. "Santo Maria della stupido." Sal was barely able to breathe but he tossed the line back gripping his end. It hit the raft with ease. "Now hold on for God's sake." Sal began slowly walking back to the shore through the muck as the two boys held on tightly. Maria refused to move. As the ground became more firm underfoot, Sal made progress.

Without a word, as the raft neared the shore, the boys jumped out and helped secure it and just as quickly untied the garments and put them on. "Thank you, Uncle

Sal." Roberto was the first to speak to an exhausted figure now sitting on a log. Sal only nodded in recognition.

Maria started to speak but Sal waved her off to address the boys. "Did you knock over the beehive when you dragged this thing? Eh, did you?" Before anyone could answer, Sal turned back to Maria. "Maria, you are wearing Roberto's shirt."

"I don't care. I have it on and it's staying on." She pursed her lips in an act of defiance.

"But Maria," Roberto, glad to talk of another topic than the beehive, said. "I'll have to wear a girl's top."

Maria glared at him. "Too bad. You shouldn't have lost the paddle trying to hit the eels."

"Eels?" Sal's eyes opened. "There are eels in this water?"

Antonio was surprised at his uncle's reaction because he had never seen his uncle afraid. "You don't like eels, Uncle Sal?"

"I love eels, especially in my marinara sauce." He smiled thinking of a meal. He then frowned turning his attention back to the boys. "But you did not answer my question about the beehive."

"I might have hit it by mistake. We were in a hurry, Uncle Sal." Antonio looked contrite having to admit the truth to the person who just saved them from disaster. "I am sorry."

"Ah, sorry. You break my hives, I get stung, you lose a paddle, and I have to walk up to my chin in that slimy water where I could have been bitten by crabs and it's 'Sorry'." He looked over to Maria. "And poor Maria has to take off her clothes so..."

"Uncle Sal, please." Maria rolled her eyes in protest.

"Okay, Okay. Va benne." He held up his hands gesturing that enough has been said. They looked at each other then the raft waiting for Sal to speak. "Where did you get the planks?"

"They were just lying in your garden doing nothing," Roberto said. He glanced at Antonio who nodded.

"Doing nothing? You mean the ones I use to divert the water so that my plants get water? Do you mean that kind of nothing?" The boys looked at each other and shrugged. "So that when I turn on the water, it will go anywhere it wants, flooding my new sprouts and Tino has to live on an island?" The boys stood accused. "And don't be too smug, Maria. Girls are supposed to have more sense than boys. You should have warned them or come to me, eh?" The three were quiet. They figured it was the best policy. "Okay. Get back to the house and get cleaned up. I'm going to stay here and take apart the raft." The three started to leave when Sal called to Antonio. "Antonio I want you to find out how to make an eel trap. Eels are good eating."

Maria looked in horror at her uncle. "Eels are like snakes, only in water."

"Bene, bene, mio caro, Maria, but they are delicious". As the kids ran back through the woods Sal pulled the raft to him to begin dismantling it. It was then that he met Dominic who had seen everything that had happened.

Chapter 3

Dominic Salutati was a chef, a scoundrel and a Sicilian. He was born in Leotini but his real home was the surrounding villages where he could get a handout or do some manual chore for change or food. This behavior was particularly strange because his father was a banker and his mother a successful realtor. He was doing it for the experience and in defiance of his parents.

Upon graduation from a private school, Dominic told his parents he wanted to be an artist and poet and so left home to wander about Europe, then South America coming to America to be a chef. By his mid-forties he had settled into a restaurant called Sprezza that was located in a section of Baltimore known as Little Italy.

The owners of the Sprezza didn't know what to make of Dominic. He prepared excellent dishes but the recipe would change according to what Dominic was buying that day. Much of his cooking was spontaneous combustion that could not be repeated. The owners complained but the patrons did not, so they allowed for his whims, his schemes and his bon vivant life.

On the day of the raft incident Dominic had come to the creek to fish, or to swim, or maybe to boat or to just do whatever came to mind. "That was quite a thing you did with the kids just now," Dominic said as he approached the drenched seated figure.

Sal who was untying the knots on the raft noticed that the twine was already beginning to unravel. In a very short time the raft would have fallen apart. 'Fate,' he thought. 'So much of life is fate. We take credit or blame for matters not in our hands even as to our birth and death.' He looked up at the approaching man. "So you saw the vaudeville, eh?" Sal asked, continuing his task.

"Do you know them?" Dominic asked as he sat near Sal on a well bleached log that looked like an upside down Dalmatian.

"Who knows children? You have any?" Sal was trying to save as much of the twine as he could, wondering where the kids had gotten so much of it. There was none in the garage that he knew of but that garage was a museum of the once useful. Giorgio had been a pack rat often making deals for haircuts or lessons. Sal had found among the debris a crank for a 1918 Ford and a headlight for a 1933 Cord. Just one.

"Me? Children?" Dominic shook his head. "Not me, I'm too independent for that." When Dominic smiled at the suggestion of parenthood he displayed a magnificent set of straight white teeth that required an egotistic attention to himself.

Sal looked toward the woods where the three had disappeared. "I know them. My sister has five more. I'm their Uncle Sal. Salvatore Pasquali. And you?" Sal extended his hand then withdrew it realizing it was slimy with water.

"Dominic Salutati." The two just nodded at each other in place of a handshake. "You sound Italian."

"Sicilian, and you?"

"Si. I'm from Leotini, near Catania. And you?"

"Cefalu in the north."

"Not too far, eh? We'd make good neighbors. We're out of gun range of each other." Dominic laughed displaying those wonderful dentures. Sal joined him in the humor that was more truthful than either would care to admit. They sat for a while just staring at the creek enjoying the coolness of the breeze.

"I'm a chef at La Sprezza in Little Italy. Ever hear of it?" Dominic continued looking at the creek.

"Sure. That's where they fry the salad, right?" Sal put the salvaged string into his pocket and began stacking the planks.

"That's right. That was my idea." He turned to Sal. "You like it?"

"I've only heard of it. Can you imagine taking all these kids to La Sprezza? It would cost a week's pay, so I made the salad myself. It wasn't bad, but I'm sure you do it a lot better." Sal realized that he'd have to come back for a second load.

"Yourself? Where did you get the recipe?" Dominic looked confused and hurt that perhaps someone at La Sprezza had betrayed him.

"It was in the paper. Look, I need to get back to my garden. Rosalina is making supper and the kids need watching as you can tell." Sal stood hefting a load of wood to his side. "We all don't have the luxury of sitting around looking at the sky. You must be single, eh?"

"Single? Of course, but what paper was that? I didn't give out the recipe." Dominic also stood. With the hair of his chest protruding from his knit shirt and his pompadour haircut, he was the personification of the

Italian playboy, especially with a golden 'horn' hanging form his neck.

"It was in the church bulletin. Rosalina brought it home and I tried it. Maybe someone who works with you also belongs to the church. I don't think the person meant any harm." Sal smiled. "Whoever it was thought it was good enough that he wanted to share it. Be complimented."

Dominic didn't like the idea of having his creations mistreated. "Home? Where is that?"

"Through these woods." Sal pointed to the single lane path. "You want to come, maybe have something to eat? It won't be La Sprezza, but were having chicken with my marinara sauce, a little fromaggio, vino, pane, and noise. You know the routine." Sal started to walk to the woods carrying about half the planks.

"What are you doing with the wood?"

"It's for my garden. I use it to divert the water." Sal glanced at the rest of the wood on the ground implying he needed Dominic's help.

"Oh, si, I used to do that at our place in Italy. My father had a gardener and I would help. Want some help?" Dominic followed Sal's eyes to the wood. "I'll get the rest of these planks." He picked them up and followed Sal.

They had just entered the shade when Sal asked, "Tell me, do you know any recipes for eel?"

"What I don't know I'm good at improvising." Dominic nodded in the direction of the path. "Avanti."

Chapter 4

Just as they cleared the woods, Sal knew that
something was not right. In the distance, past the hives
and the coop and the well he saw clothes strewn over the
bushes and even on the large doll house. The two men
looked at each other, put down the planks near the spring
house and walked toward where Yolanda and Mama were
putting out the laundry.

As they passed the coop, Rolando, who was feeding the
chickens from a large yellow bucket, called out, "Uncle
Sal, who is your friend?"

Sal wondered what Rolando was feeding the chickens
since the feed came in a metal bucket. "This is Mr.
Salutati. He's a chef from an important restaurant in the
city."

"Dominic, please," interrupted his guest.

Sal nodded. "Bene. This is Dominic and Dominic this is
my Rolando who is feeding the chickens the garlic I had
crushed." He turned to Dominic. "That way, you see, the
spice is already in the meat." He then turned back to

Rolando. "Why are Yolanda and your mother throwing the clothes all over the place?"

"Someone stole the clothesline." Rolando stopped his chore. "Hi, Mr. Dominic, are you staying for dinner? I hope Antonio gets back. He said that he had something very important to do for Uncle Sal."

"Hi, Rolando. So you like birds, eh? So do I, but I don't feed them, they feed me." Dominic smiled at his own pun.

"I like birds that fly. Chickens are too heavy so they just walk around and eat. They can't even fly over the fence."

"So they're easy to catch and eat, right?" Dominic said.

"Only if you don't give them a name." Rolando came through the gate.

Sal listened to Rolando and Dominic but his mind was on why anyone would want to steal a clothesline. Then he realized; it was to make a raft. "Where is Roberto? Did he go with Antonio?"

"No, Uncle Sal, he's with Samuel." Rolando pointed in the direction of the flagpole where three year old Samuel was attached to the pole by a large loop of wire. It allowed Sam to freely move about in a fifteen foot circle and playing with him in the dirt was Roberto.

"Sal," it was Rosalina. "Someone has taken our clothesline. Who would do such a thing?"

Sal only shook his head. "I think there's more in the garage. I'll get it." He knew he'd walk into the garage, take the twine from his pocket and pretend he found it. Why cause a problem?

Just as Sal started toward the garage, Dominic held him back gently with a tug at Sal's shoulder. "What is that, Sal?" He pointed to a small marble cross in the center of which was a small picture of a very young girl.

Sal looked at Dominic, the cross, then back to Dominic. "That's Rosalina's little girl, Theresa. She died of a fever when she was almost two."

"So you buried her here?" Dominic kept staring, not believing anyone could bury their family in their yard.

"I didn't. Giorgio and Rosalina did. I was still in Sicily."

"Giorgio is Rosalina's husband?"

"Was. He died about three years ago. He's over there near the stream. This whole area, including my own plot, is for the family. Part of life, eh?"

"So Rosalina is a widow."

"Si, and with eight children."

Dominic stood in thought looking at the area. "What kind of fever? What did the doctor say?"

"Doctor? They're expensive when you have no insurance. The coroner put down pneumonia, but it wasn't. She's gone." Sal looked deeply into Dominic's eyes. "She was loved. She is missed, but there are many mouths to feed, clothes to wash and... well just and." For a brief moment the two men just looked at the cross. "So much of life is fate." Sal said. "So much."

"And Giorgio?" Dominic looked toward the larger stone.

"An automobile accident. He was a hardworking, caring man. They loved each other very much. She followed him to America and had nine children." Then with a deep sigh, Sal forced a smile to change the topic. "Would you care for some espresso?"

When Sal gave Rosalina the twine she asked "Where did you get this? It is wet."

"It was at the bottom of some stuff," Sal said glancing at Dominic.

"And who is this?" Rosalina asked finally noticing Dominic.

"This is Dominic. He's a chef at La Sprezza in Little Italy. He likes to fry his salads. This is my sister, Rosalina, who likes to throw our clothes over the lawn."

"Boungiorno, pleased to meet..."

"Mama," Roberto interrupted with a yell. "Samuel won't listen to me." He turned to his younger brother. "I told you not to pull on the wire. Stop it, Samuel, stop." He faced his mom. "See, he won't listen."

Rosalina turned from the boys to face Dominic. "Scusi, but we'll talk later. You will stay for dinner, yes?"

"Sure, maybe I can help? I can be useful in the kitchen." Dominic liked the way Rosalina cared.

Rosalina nodded as she walked to the boys saying, "Anything you can do will be helpful." She stopped and said to Sal, "Please get the man something to drink, eh?" She raised her right hand palm up to the sky as if saying what can you do?

Yolanda and Rolando took the twine and began repairing the clothesline as the two men went inside. Descending the stairs to the kitchen Dominic noticed the pictures mounted on the wall that had the name Yolanda on them. One, which at first Dominic thought was a print, was particularly good having a touch of Van Gogh. "This picture is very good. Who is Yolanda?"

"Yolanda is the oldest. She was hanging the clothes with Rosalina, her mother. She has a great deal of her grandmother, Beatrice, in her in liking art, but she is shy. One day, who knows, eh?"

"And where is her grandmother?" Dominic asked as they entered a small room that had an old sofa, a T.V., and a bunch of pots with herbs near a sunny window. The room did not have a rug or curtains or wallpaper.

"Our parents are still in Sicily near Cefalu. He's a barber and does odd jobs when he can work and my mother, who would like to travel, works the garden. She's an excellent artist. She redesigned the mayor's residence." Sal had reached a doorway covered by some cloth and motioned for his guest to enter.

Dominic noticed a vase with some flowers where a T.V. screen should have been. "What happened here?" He pointed at the set.

Sal looked at the set then Dominic." One of the kids, Antonio, broke the screen with a baseball bat and so we put a flower there." He shrugged. Things like that were normal.

"Why don't you fix it?"

"We will one day but no one seems to miss it. They have too many things to do. They have too much trouble to get into." Sal motioned again for Dominic to go to the kitchen. "Rosalina prefers the radio. That way she can listen as she works. With the television she has to stop and watch what is going on. Beside, the radio has more music and Rosalina loves music. It was one of the appeals of Giorgio."

Sal followed Dominic into a large kitchen area that had a long wooden table with benches on the side and two chairs at the ends. It could accommodate twelve people. It was neat, but poor. The place smelled of garlic, oregano, and cheese. On a side table, under a window, was a large bottle of generic red wine, cans of olive oil, cans of tomato paste, boxes of pasta, and a bowl of fresh vegetables. On the stove was a large pot of boiling water where the chicken was cooking. Above the sink hung various size pots and pans and on a shelf between the stove and sink, strategically placed for ready use was an assortment of knives that appeared well maintained.

To one side of the table was a young heavy set girl who was slowly grating cheese perhaps in preparation for that night's meal. "Nothing tastes better than freshly grated cheese," said Dominic. "Even though I can get others to grate, I do my own. What kind of cheese do you have?"

The girl looked up to Sal ignoring the guest. Sal smiled at her. "Dominic, this is Maria. Maria, this is Dominic. He is a chef and he will be our guest tonight."

Maria then spoke. "This is Parmesan. You can't grate mozzarella or provolone. What kind do you use?" She took a pinch of cheese and ate it.

"Not too much, Maria, Okay?" said Sal getting the espresso maker.

"I sometimes use Romano in certain meals but Parmesan, especially Reggiano, is the best." Dominic took one of the heels of the cheese and began chewing it. "Good calcium and better than candy."

"Have we ever had Reginald cheese, Uncle Sal?" Maria did not like the idea of someone taking her cheese.

"No, Maria, that's a little too rich for us, but what we have, is very good." Sal glanced at his guest. "Do you like your coffee strong?"

"Yes." Dominic went over to the knives and closely examined them. "These are an excellent set, and they look old. Who sharpens them?"

"I do. I also do the repairs, tend the garden, watch the kids, and try to squeeze in some construction for money. And yes, they are very old with an interesting story that involves the Turks. One day, perhaps I'll tell you about it."

"Turks?" Dominic looked surprised.

"It's not for young ears," Sal nodded toward Maria. As he talked Sal filled the octagon coffee pot with water, filled the small canister with deep brown powder, screwed everything together and placed it on the stove. In a few moments the place filled with the scent of coffee.

Chapter 5

Sal handed Dominic a small cup of espresso and a biscotti. "Tell me about your people back in Italy. I believe you said you were from Leotini near Catania?"

Dominic heard him and continued looking about the room taking in the picture of Jesus painted directly on the wall and a beautiful mural of a Renaissance garden on another wall. Hung on one side of the door was a mandolin and on the other side, two badminton rackets. In a corner of the room were some work boots encrusted with cement, and in another corner a pile of art books. There were vases of flowers on the sink and table and a two foot enameled urn with a lion motif held open a door that led to a back room. Though a ceiling was absent, the exposed rafters had been painted, and stuffed in various places in these rafters were magazines or papers that still needed to be read. He could hear the pot boiling, the soft swish of cheese on the grater and far away and above him a song from a radio that someone may have forgotten to turn off.

He compared the practical coffee maker of his host with the elaborate three thousand dollar one at La Sprezza.

"Dominic," Sal said, "Do you like lemon or sugar?"

"Oh, sure." Dominic whetted his lips as he took a bite of the biscotti. "Well, my people are there in Italy being bankers and big money makers. They're not like me at all. So I left..."

"Oh my God, "Rosalina burst into the room carrying Samuel, making Maria drop some cheese she was about to eat. "Do you know what this child did? No, of course you don't. He stuffed his ears with dirt. That's why he couldn't listen to Roberto. Dirt in the ears. Oh, Madonna di Christo. Why? Why?" She screamed at the child who could not hear her, making him frightened. His look of confusion would have been amusing in another circumstance.

"Rosalina, the child can't hear you, but the rest of us can. Here, give me Samuel." Dominic hurriedly got out of the way of Yolanda, Rolando, Roberto, Francesca, and Josephine who wanted to see what was happening. Sal brought the nervous child to the sink, turned on the warm water and slowly squirted some into Samuel's left ear. Muddy water started to flow out.

"Is he going to be alright?" asked Yolanda.

"Is he going to the hospital?" asked Francesca as she scrambled to a chair then on to the table next to Maria. Rolando only stood and watched wishing he would have known what to do, whereas Josephine kept close to her mother.

Dominic came over to Sal. "He is going to be alright, isn't he?"

"Si, hold him still, Dominic, I don't want to spray water in his eyes. He's very frightened about all this attention." He gave his sister a stern look.

"Everybody," Rosalina spoke up as on cue. "Out, now. Wait outside so the doctor can do his job. It's outside or everyone gets castor oil."

Dominic, holding Samuel's feet still, quickly turned in disbelief to what he had heard, but it was Yolanda who asked, "Oh, Mama, why do you give us all castor oil when one of us is sick?" As she spoke she removed Francesca from the table and began scurrying the others with her except for Maria.

Mama noticed Maria. "And no cheese for you at dinner, you've had enough for three people." She grabbed the bowl of grated cheese and nodded for her to leave. "And as far as you, Yolanda, when you get married some day, how I'll never know because you don't even date, you'll understand. Now take them out. Give your uncle some quiet. What kind of impression are we making on our guest who has not even had time to drink his coffee?"

"Coffee?" Sal looked up at his sister, "Rosalina, see if Dominic would want more."

"I'll get it," said Dominic.

Rosalina got to the pot first. "If you don't mind, guests in my house don't serve themselves. Sit down so I can be a good host. Do you want sugar?"

"And lemon, if you don't mind," said Dominic as he sat.

Rosalina mechanically prepared the drink glancing over at Samuel then handed it to Dominic. "There. Is everything okay?" Before the man could answer, Rosalina called out to Sal. "Is Samuel okay?"

"Mama," Samuel turned toward his mother. "Why is Unca Sal putting water in my ears?"

"He's washing out your ears, stupido."

"Why is he washing my ears?"

"Because you..." She stopped. "He can hear me. The boy can hear me." She moved toward the two at the sink.

"Of course he can hear you, Rosalina. All the neighbors can hear you," Sal said. "Now for the other ear. Dominic, I still could use some help. Rosalina, could you turn down the chicken?" Dominic wolfed down his drink and joined Sal at the sink.

"Oh," Rosalina said turning down the heat. "Not only are you a doctor, you want to be a chef, eh? Okay, what do you want done with the chicken?"

Dominic held the boy's legs steady as he peered into the pot. "You should skim off the froth that would give it a bitter taste, add about eight bay leaves, and press the bird so that it will absorb the juices. In about fifteen minutes I would add a bouquet garni..." He stopped to look at Sal and Rosalina, "which would give it a..." Dominic noticed they were both staring at him.".....a provincial flavor, but simmering would do for now."

"Who are you?" asked Rosalina. "Did you enjoy the coffee?"

"Yes, very much, and the biscotti. Thank you." He released the boy and faced Rosalina. "So your husband and your father enjoyed music as you do. So do I. As a matter of fact I can play the mandolin."

"That's good," Rosalina said taking Samuel from Sal. "Now listen to me. Can you hear me?"

"Yes, Mama."

"Good. Never put dirt in your ears, again. Understand?" She kissed him on the cheek.

"Okay, Mama."

Rosalina reached up and brought down a box of Torrone candy and gave him one, then several more. "Give everybody a piece of candy. Now go play and no dirt in the ears." Samuel, clutching his treasure, rushed out to share.

Sal washed his hands then said, "I have a garden to tend and you, Rosalina have a dinner to cook."

"And when anybody wants some candy," said Dominic, "all they have to do is stuff their ears with dirt."

"The next time," Rosalina said with a frown," the dirt will be knocked out, not washed out." She turned to Dominic. "How come you know so much about cooking?"

"I'm a chef."

"A chef?"

"Would you like me to show you?" His smile was more of a smirk.

"Go ahead, chef, show us. It'll give me some time to clean the rooms."

"I'll have to make some special purchases but everything will be done on time."

"Special purchases?" Rosalina looked at Dominic with caution. "We do without special purchases."

"My treat."

"Then make all the special purchases you want."

That night the family was treated to a dinner so exquisite that it would be talked about for years. It would be remembered not only for the refined taste of Marsala di capanata di Campi con pasta, not only for the sweet flavor of eight year old Reggiano Parmesan, but also for the delicacy of Tuscany's Ducale Rusticana Chianti, and also Antonio's contribution.

Chapter 6

Dinner was the only time the family sat together to eat except on rare occasions when pranzo (lunch) was the main meal. The rest of the time people ate what and when they could, under the watchful eye of Mama and Sal. Bread with sauce or olive oil for dipping was fine, but cheese and pepperoni were allotted. One was allowed to eat whatever fruit was available but sweets were restricted. At the main meal, Mama would always serve while Uncle Sal gave out the cheese and pepperoni by seniority or how much work had been done. Wine was dosed out by age with mostly water for Francesca, Josephine and Rolando, none for the baby and all wine for Sal. Usually the meal was pasta served with a meat sauce, mostly chicken. On some occasions, there was seafood but rarely veal. One day Sal had brought home an entire pig he had accidentally killed with his car. The owner, in lieu of repairing the fender, gave Sal the pig because it was his fault that the pig was loose. There still was a large dent in the right fender, but they ate sausage for many meals.

After everyone sat down for dinner, Mama personally checked each one for cleanliness. Dominic set the plate of delicious Marsala chicken in the middle of the table. Marsala was a new smell to everyone though that wine was native to Sicily. Marsala was an expensive treat and neither Mama nor Sal cooked with it. Mama said a prayer basically hoping that no one would get sick, that our guest was a friend, and that we should thank the guest for cooking and sharing. She prayed for Yolanda to find a nice boy, for Antonio to do better in school, for Roberto to be not so lazy, for Maria to lose weight, for Francesca and Josephine to listen to authority, for Rolando to not do dangerous things, for Sam to be healthy, and for Sal for being such a good brother. She ended the prayer with, "Your will be done, you know I've done my best."

During the prayer Dominic looked around the room once again. He wondered if they would like his meal because it was different than what they were used to. A meal like this would easily cost thirty to forty dollars a plate at La Sprezza, but then at La Sprezza, it would be served by tux clad waiters with an ambiance of crystal, lace, and linen. Everyone said amen except Dominic. They sat in silence waiting.

"Is there something wrong?" asked Dominic. "Do I have the right music?" (In the background a Sicilian serenade was playing,on his disk player) "Eh?" He looked around for an answer.

Sal spoke up. "We are waiting for you to serve."

"Me?" He picked up the bowl and passed it to his left. "Here, mangiano." He handed the bowl to Rosalina.

Rosalina gave the bowl back gently. "Here, we pass our plates to the server. That way what is given is fair. Let me show you." She stood. She reached out to Sal. "Sal, you are first." Each person in turn handed Mama their plate and each was given a portion according to the ancient way of eldest first, worker first. As each person received back their plate filled with the new taste treat, Sal picked up the grated cheese and put some on each plate. When everyone was served, and as they began to eat, the chatter started as they enjoyed the meal.

"And there is plenty for seconds," said Dominic.

"What is Marsala?" asked Yolanda of Dominic.

"A sweet wine of western Sicily."

"How did you make the chicken so juicy?"

"You have to squeeze it at the right time."

"This is very sweet cheese," said Antonio.

"What are the little green berries?" asked Josephine.

"They are called capers. They come from a little tree."

In the middle of all this eating and talking, Josephine, who was sitting next to Dominic, asked him, "How come you didn't pray?" This question got Sal and Rosalina's attention which in turn made the others silent.

"Oh, but I did pray."

"You didn't close your eyes or bow your head."

Dominic looked at the others who were listening to him. "Everyone has their way of praying. Some people stand, some bow, some sit, some sing, and some even dance. I cook. My prayer is my cooking. I hope the people like it but I hope that God likes it too."

Josephine looked down at her plate thinking, then looked up at Dominic. "Okay."

Rosalina looked up at her guest. "This is a very good meal, Dominic. You are a good chef. Are you Catholic?"

"Thank you, Rosalina, but no, I'm not a Catholic. Of course, I was raised Catholic. I'm Sicilian, but life has a way of changing things." Dominic looked at Sal in a 'You know what I mean' look.

"So you don't go to church," Rosalina casually said as she had more sauce.

"No, I don't," said Dominic putting down his fork. "May I ask...?"

"But you believe in God, right?" Rosalina only glanced at him.

"Rosalina, everyone has his own idea of God. My God is a grand chef who is trying to teach me how to cook a good life. I'm not the best learner but I recognize his authority. I have learned something. When you cook, with passionati, you can make a lot of mistakes and it will turn out fine. It's like music. You can know the notes perfectly but be a bad player. Like in art," he looked at Yolanda. "You can have the right composition but there is no life in the picture. You have to put life into the notes, passion into the paint, and spirit into the sauce. My parents have made a great deal of money but they have no real wealth. Their life is a beautiful tomb." There was silence as each person thought about what was said. Rosalina dipped some bread into the sauce to give Samuel. She was 'moying'—a Sicilian slang for sopping. Even Sal was 'moying'.

"Are you Catholic, Rosalina?" Dominic asked.

"No." There was silence again.

"May I ask...?" Dominic began but Sal reached over and gently touched his hand. When Dominic looked over he saw Sal shaking his head.

"It concerns Theresa," Sal said softly.

"There is no need to whisper," said Rosalina. "Ever since that time, I've gone to the Pentecostal church. We don't talk about death there. We sing and pray and help each other. There are a lot of unfortunate people but they are all good." Rosalina looked at the children eating around the table. "We try to help sometimes, eh?" Everyone nodded their approval.

"I decorated eggs for the church this year," said Francesca.

"I collected bags of food," added Josephine.

"I helped Josephine," chimed in Rolando.

"And Roberto and Maria," Rosalina said smiling at the two, "have done chores for the elderly of the church and Yolanda has tutored some of the kids after school."

Dominic looked at each person as they were mentioned, then looked at Sal. "What about you?"

"I do my share."

"You don't sound too happy about it." Dominic leaned back in his chair.

"It's not always pleasant to do God's will."

"You need a drink of this excellent Chianti," Dominic reached down to the bottle beside his chair. Looking up at Rosalina, he asked, "How about Rosalina?"

"Just a small bit and I add water." Rosalina extended her glass.

"And the workers of God's will?" Dominic looked at the children.

The kids were ready but Mama said, "Only Yolanda this evening and she too will have water."

Dominic turned to Antonio. "I haven't heard what you do. Do you help with the church?"

"Well...I...don't really like those..." He turned from Dominic and noticed a bag in the sink. "I forgot to show Uncle Sal what I got for him." He grabbed the bag pulling it toward the table. "I got all these for free." The wet bag broke spilling onto the table, floor, and people, four dozen live eels. There was an instant explosion of activity, screams and yells.

The first to react was Yolanda who leapt from her chair to the table kicking not only eels, but food in all directions. Rosalina grabbed Samuel and Josephine dragging them as they screamed to the T.V. room. There she roughly deposited them on the sofa with a stern direction to

Josephine to watch the baby. In her excitement Rosalina often used Italian words confusing the girl.

Francesca joined her older sister on the table top adding her own screams while Antonio and Roberto took up arms in the form of badminton rackets to defend the family from invasion by bashing and scooping the eels.

Uncle Sal, at first dazed by the event, got up to get a large pot to scoop, stepped on an eel, slipped, and fell against Dominic who was still stunned by having eels dumped on him and his dinner. As the two men hit the floor surrounded by slithering creatures, Antonio, seeing his uncle down, tried to scoop the enemy away but only managed to jab the racket into Sal's nose and drive an eel down Dominic's shirt.

Maria in her confused state ran for the fire extinguisher thinking the spray would kill the beasts. Her aim was bad, striking Dominic in the chest, and then having lost control of the device sprayed everywhere.

Dominic, having been hit by Sal, by Antonio, by eels, and by Maria struggled to his feet to save what he could of his meal, but stepping on something slimy and squished fell again, this time with a pot of pasta. With no hands to brace his fall Dominic hit the sink and was knocked out.

Sal, seeing his guest sprawled on the floor covered in spray, pasta and eels with a nasty welt on his head dragged the man to the safety of his bedroom next to the kitchen.

At that moment Rosalina re-entered the room, grabbed Maria and the extinguisher and yelled at Yolanda. "Get off the table. What's wrong with you? They're only eels for God's sake. Now shut up, all of you. Look at Francesca at the sink. She is playing with them. Yolanda set a good..." Rosalina stopped in her tirade to notice the room. "Oh, my God, look at this mess. Antonio and Roberto stop hitting them. Go get the gloves so you can pick them up. Go. Go."

She looked around. "Where is Uncle Sal?" She heard some noise behind her. It was Yolanda shaking with fear humming some tune that was unrecognizable. "Yolanda?"

"Si, Mama." Yolanda seemed dazed.

"Go in the next room and take care of the children. There are no eels there, eh?" Yolanda nodded and left. Rosalina thought of what she was going to do with a girl who was scared of anything that looked like a snake.

Sal came in to the room. "Dominic was knocked out but he'll be fine. Where is Rolando? He likes to help."

"Rolando can wait," Rosalina said. "Right now, scoop."

Within a short time the eels were in the sink and Sal drank the last bit of Chianti from a turned over bottle. "This is really good wine, Rosalina."

"Si, and a very good meal. I wonder what he planned for dessert?" Rosalina looked over at Francesca at the sink. "You like them?"

"They don't belong here. They need to go home. See, many of them are dead." Francesca continued watching them.

"Mr. Dominic," Rolando said as he came out of the bedroom, "is getting up. I washed his cut and put a bandage on it. He said he had a headache so I gave him an aspirin. Was that alright?"

Sal spoke. "That was fine. Where were you? I looked all over."

"I guess I got scared and ran off. Sorry." There was something missing in the boy's tone. It was truth. Sal decided to let it go for now.

"Antonio," Sal squinted at the boy, "how many eels did you have?"

"Four dozen."

"Four dozen? I count only thirty-nine. Are you sure it was four dozen. That's forty-eight, not thirty-nine."

"There was four dozen," Antonio insisted. "I counted them when Rudolpho put them in the bag."

"Then there are nine missing. I don't want to find them by my nose. Now what? Look." They looked but found nothing. "Where did you say you got these?"

"Mr. Minnick has a friend, Rudolpho. He fishes off East Island where he says there are a lot of eels." He started to put the badminton racket on the wall.

"I know him." Sal said, "Antonio, please wash the thing first, okay? That man is a hard worker."

"He says he knows you because he goes to Mama's church. When I told him you wanted eels to eat he said he had plenty. They get in the way of crabbing, except as bait. He said I could have all I wanted for cleaning his boat once a week."

Antonio was going to say more but Dominic emerged from Sal's room. He held his head with a small band-aid and leaned against the wall. He looked terrible. His hair was tossed, his shirt was ripped with large stains, his pants had a torn pocket, and his shoes had slimy eel parts hanging from them. He just stood there.

Sal stared at first then asked, "Would you care for some espresso?"

Dominic answered in a fog. "Espresso? Sure, why not. I have some pastry in the refrigerator if the eels didn't get it. Where is Rosalina? I won't ask what happened I'll just tell my psychiatrist and he'll tell me."

Chapter 7

The next morning, shrouded in a light mist, promised a day of heat so Mama prepared a cool breakfast called popadillo. This Sicilian meal consisted of warm sweet milk poured over raisin toast and the mixture allowed to cool between two bowls, one inverted over the other. At five-thirty, though, only Sal, Rosalina and Rolando were up. The others would wake soon and Yolanda would be in charge.

"Did you know," Sal said, "that Dominic's shirt cost three hundred dollars? That his pants cost about the same? And so did his shoes? Can you imagine wearing over a thousand dollars worth of clothes for everyday wear?"

"I can imagine all sorts of things but what else does he pay for?" Rosalina went to the sink to clean the dishes.

"And he has rich parents," added Sal.

"Sal, when are you going to get these dead eels out of here?"

"Dead? Rolando raced to the sink to see thirty-two dead eels and seven moving sluggishly. "Why are they dead?"

"I guess it's not their kind of water. Eels like all that slime to swim in. We have well water like everyone else on our block," explained Sal. Rolando looked depressed.

A scream, which did not come from the house, pierced the morning calm. It came from the Strassmyers, across the street. Another scream then hurried, panicky voices. Sal and Rosalina stared at each other thinking that Bruno, the crazy dog, had gotten loose and attacked one of the neighbors. They knew that one day it would happen. Sal gulped his coffee then went to the door. He turned to Rolando. "Want to go with me?"

"I don't think so."

"Somebody could be hurt." Sal encouraged him.

Rolando moved reluctantly. "Okay, but I hope nobody is." Just as they were leaving they could hear stirrings upstairs as the others got dressed to see what had happened. Sal and Rolando were crossing the street when a police car pulled up.

The Strassmyers had money. He managed a large department store downtown for whom Sal had done some cement work. The Strassmyers paid people to do their lawn, often their laundry, and any repairs around the house. They had a swimming pool, central air, a new car, and every new gadget possible whether they needed it or not. It wasn't the use that was important, it was the purchasing. They also had a twelve year old daughter named Tracy, but who was often called Princess. It was from Tracy they heard the screams. Sal and Rolando moved close enough to the police that they could learn of the problem, yet remain not a part of it.

"And when did you discover these eels in your pool, Mr. Strassmyer?" asked the heavier officer as mother and daughter clutched each other in the background.

Tracy answered. "As soon as I came out to get an early swim. I can't stand the heat or the direct sun. And there they were, those disgusting things in my clean pool."

"I called Ken Baldwin, your boss," blurted in Mr. Strassmyer, "and he told me he'd send someone pronto."

"We got here as soon as we could, Mr. Strassmyer," said the thinner officer hoisting up his belt that carried a revolver.

"You got here fine, Officer, I'll be sure to tell Ken." He was more pleased with his power over the police than in any efficiency on their part. "Anyway, these creatures were in the pool. They were all dead except one and I bashed its head in. I can't figure how they got in the pool."

Rolando turned his head away at the news of the bashing and Sal held him close.

"How many were there?" asked the big cop.

"Nine. There were nine, but what I...' Strassmyer went on.

Sal said to Rolando, "I don't think we need to hear more. That accounts for them all. They will spend the rest of the day draining and cleaning the pool. Then they'll talk about it because that's their life, talk." He looked at Rolando. "But we know what happened, don't we?"

Rolando nodded. "I tried to save them, but they were going to die no matter what I did, right, Uncle Sal?"

"I think so. So much of life, Rolando, is just chance. Almost out of our control." Sal spoke softly as they returned to their house.

"So what's the problem with the Strassmyers?" asked Rosalina. The rest of the family was now up and eating. They all wanted to hear the news.

"It seems the Strassmyers don't like eels in their pool," Sal reached for more coffee. It was not even six-thirty and it felt like a full day.

"Why not?" asked Francesca. "What's wrong with eels?"

"My eels in their swimming pool?" asked Antonio.

"And when did they become your eels?" asked Roberto.

Yolanda was about to say something when Mama raised her hand to silence her. "That is not the point. How did those eels get in there?" Sal looked at Rolando and the others followed his gaze.

"You put the eels in there?" asked Maria. "Why?"

"I wanted them to live. We took them from their nice home and we were mean to them." Rolando looked at the family. "I just wanted them to live."

Mama was about to speak when Yolanda spoke up. "He's right, Mama. He just wanted to help."

"Maybe," Antonio said, "we should bring the rest of the eels over." He smiled imagining the reaction of the neighbors.

"I don't think that's a very good idea, Antonio," Sal shook his head. "Right now the Strassmyers are confused. I don't want them to think we did it."

"But we did do it," said Josephine.

"Yes, I know that, we all know that, but I don't want them to know that," Sal tried to explain.

"Why not?" asked Francesca.

Sal looked at his sister. He knew the Strassmyers did not like them. They did not like any Italians. They did not like anyone who was not them. How do you explain bigotry to a child? Sal continued, "They will get angry and they will yell and they will make Rolando do a lot of work like cleaning the pool on a hot day. We know Rolando is too young to clean that pool so we would all have to help including Mama who would not cook lasagna for tonight. We would all have to eat oatmeal with cod liver oil."

"So, if we lie," Yolanda frowned, "we get away with it, eh?"

"If we just keep quiet," Sal said, "they can spend a little of all that money they took from hard working people. Beside, Mr. Strassmyer never paid me for that back sidewalk. So there." Sal grabbed the orange juice that Josephine had put her rejected popadillo in, and drank it, thinking it was his coffee. Only when he had swallowed it did he realize it was not his espresso. What it was he did not know but it was lumpy and bitter. He tried to spit out what he had already eaten. "Oh my God, what was that?" He looked around the room then at the glass in his hand. "What is this?"

"That's my orange juice with popadillo," said Josephine wondering why her uncle wanted it.

Sal looked around at the family staring back at him. "Well, at least it wasn't eel juice, eh?" Sal forced a weak smile.

Everyone started to laugh including Yolanda who gave up trying to make her point. "This family is nuts. Maybe," she turned to her mother, "maybe I'm nervous about bringing Marcello here."

The laughter came to an abrupt end as Mama was taken back. "Marcello? And who is this Marcello? Have we met him before?" She turned to Sal. "Have you heard of Marcello?" Before he could answer, she looked at the rest of the family. "Has anyone heard of Marcello?" She looked at Yolanda. "Is that his first or last name?"

Yolanda took a deep breath. "It's his first name, Mama, and you know him. He plays the piano at the church. Marcello Bacci. He not only plays music he is going to college to get a degree in music. He also likes to paint."

"Oh?" Mama said continuing to listen.

"He is a good student and he's on the soccer team. He lives in the nice Sarasota neighborhood. He has a brother, two sisters and his mother's people are from Capua near

Naples. They import Italian foods. They own the Tivoli Grocery Store."

Mama leaned forward placing her elbows on the table. "You seem to know a lot about this Marcello. How long has this been going on?"

"What do you mean by this? I..." she looked around at the smiling faces, "I talked to him a few times and I thought you might like to meet him."

"Yes, I would like to meet him," Mama said. "I'd like to hear what kind of music he plays. Please, bring Marcello to dinner. We can show him what a good family you come from. He'll have a good time."

"I don't think Mr. Dominic had a good time, Mama?" said Maria.

"Maria," Mama turned to her. "Clean up the dishes, put them in the sink for Yolanda to do and get a bucket of water with soap and a scrub brush. I want all the bathrooms upstairs scrubbed, and that will be done before lunch. It was pesto you wanted for lunch, eh? Yes, it was. So first you earn it." Maria started to object. "No, work first, then complain." Maria's shoulders sagged but she picked up the plates as Yolanda helped. "What are you planning today, Sal?"

"Next week I have a big job building Freeman's wall for his store," Sal shook his head. "I wish I had another pair of hands."

"Marcello knows about construction," Yolanda said.

"He does?" Sal looked up.

"He put in his father's patio."

Sal looked impressed. "That's good. Tell him to come around. I could use him. A patio?"

"Yes, with stone in it and also a wall."

"Stone? Wall? I'm impressed. And he is still in school?"

"He's a senior next year." Yolanda started to do the dishes with Maria.

Sal turned to Rosalina. "Today, Antonio is going to help me in the garden and repair the beehive. Roberto will begin painting the garage with the paint I found inside, and Rolando will feed the chickens and water all the plants. Right now I want to shave."

Chapter 8

When Sal entered the upstairs bathroom, he noticed that something was not quite right but he washed and began stropping his straight razor that once belonged to his grandfather, Taddeo. Sal loved the sound of the swish as he sharpened the blade. It was a slow process but it was relaxing. He had not only watched his father shave himself, but also many others in the village. The smell of a barbershop was his heritage. He had seen men totally transformed in less than an hour under his father's hands.

First, was the exchange of friendly words as the person entered the shop. The pace was slow because if he were in a hurry he wouldn't have come to get a haircut. A striped sheet was placed around the body bound at the neck with a soft tissue between the neck and the sheet and more friendly words. The hair would be combed gently to see what needed to be done, and then a small spray of water would be used to tame the loose ends. The cutting would begin with a scissors or sometimes a razor depending on what was done or who the person was. Movement was always slow and deliberate while the conversation would drift: investments, sports, family, weather, local gossip, certain personalities, and on rare occasions something personal. No one really expected advice from the barber, only a willing ear. All the while, the routine of trimming continued, culminating in a dose of refreshing hair tonic.

If a shave was ordered, there was another litany. First the gentle massage of the face as the customer was reclined followed by a heated towel. After the face had been prepared, his father would apply a heated shaving cream that was dispensed from a large machine that looked like an espresso maker. Again, with delicate care the well honed razor would be applied to clear the face of its stubble. A bracing tonic would be placed on the smooth face followed by a brief but important massage of the neck and shoulders. There was a yielding of oneself to those who knew their trade, and in that yielding one became more than what one was before entering. All of this was in Sal's mind as he stropped.

"Why do you do that with your razor, Uncle Sal?" asked Rolando who had been staring at his uncle.

"Oh, Rolando, I didn't see you. Don't you have some chores to do?" Sal finished his stropping.

"I have to feed the chickens, but I like watching you. Will I shave one day?" Rolando sat on the hamper.

"Yes, and sooner than you think."

"Does it hurt?"

"Not if you do it right." Sal mixed the lavender smelling soap in his shaving cup with a brush. It began to foam. "I strop my razor to get it sharp. The sharper it is, the easier to shave."

"Have you ever cut yourself?"

"Certainly, but it's usually because I wasn't paying attention, like when I talk to someone while I'm shaving."

Rolando remained silent as he watched his uncle put on the soap and shave making contortions of the face to reach more difficult spots. "Antonio used the curtain to wipe himself this morning. See." Rolando pointed to where the curtain had been placed into the toilet.

Sal turned abruptly in surprise to look at the scene. This was what was different; a curtain rammed into a toilet and flushed. "Why would Antonio...Ouch. O dio, perche? Why?" Sal looked in the mirror to see a knick that was beginning to bleed.

"You cut yourself, Uncle Sal," Rolando said staring at the blood. "Does it hurt?"

"Yes, it hurts. Yes, I cut myself, but why did Antonio wipe himself with the curtain?"

"He had no toilet paper."

"So he used the curtain, eh?" Sal washed his face of the lather. He'd shave later though he looked awkward only with his right side shaved. He applied alum to the cut and though it hurt it stopped the bleeding. He went over to the toilet and pulled out the curtain to reveal a small brown smudge.

From the doorway Maria said, "I have to clean in here." She then noticed the stain. "What's that?"

"That's where Antonio wiped himself," Rolando volunteered.

"He pooped on the curtain? I'm not cleaning that," Maria pouted in defiance.

"Of course you don't have to clean it, Maria." Sal removed the curtain and put it in the sink where he ran hot water and the lather from his cup on the spot. He rubbed the area briskly. "There. It is all gone. Now we need to get some toilet paper up here because we are running out of curtains." He smiled then noticed Maria's stare. "What is it, Maria?"

"Only half your face has hair."

"Maria, do the bathroom and Rolando come with me." Sal threw the curtain into the hamper.

"Are you going to yell at Antonio? Mama would then give him castor oil." Rolando said, following his uncle.

"Just the thing to do to a person who did that. No, I am not going to yell. I am going to tell him to stop using the curtains as toilet paper, to not poke people's eyes out, to not hit people when they sleep, and not to run over old people. Come. Vienne qui. You must feed the chickens and I have to select one for dinner."

Chapter 9

The construction of irrigation ditches with proper drainage and well fitted gates took time. At first Antonio liked the work, but after awhile Sal could see the boy's attention was drifting, often looking at the woods. "Antonio?"

"Yes?" Antonio stopped to pay attention.

"Get me a cup of water from the barrel, then I think we've done enough work for one day in the garden. You and Roberto can go play in the woods, but tell him to clean the brushes before he goes, understand?" Most of the work had been done, but Sal knew he had to make pesto and get other things ready so he could take the time to build Freeman's wall

The large pottery cup Sal held in his hand had a face that looked like the sun with little legs and arms protruding from it. Sal drank the cool water feeling the sweat run down his cheeks and back. There was something in labor that was a reward in itself. The water quenched a thirst of hard work in the heat. He looked at Antonio then at the sky. "Grazie."

A deep growl and throaty bark came from somewhere to the right. The sound filled the woods. It was a fearful, hateful sound that came from Bruno, a mastiff, owned by the Crepiscus, a family of Romanian immigrants.

Antonio quickly glanced about. "That's Bruno, isn't it?"

"Yes. That is a mean dog. I hope it never breaks loose because nobody would stand a chance against that animal. It's like the story by Sherlock Homes. The big dog attacks people at night and eats them. Then Signor Homes kills it."

"Kills who?' questioned Rolando as he walked up to the two. "Who is going to get killed?"

"Bruno," said Antonio. "Uncle Sal said that if Bruno attacks we have to get Signor Homes to kill it."

"Who is Signor Homes?" asked Rolando.

"He lives in England. If Bruno attacks we have to do it ourselves," Sal said wiping his brow.

"Would you kill him, Uncle Sal?" asked Rolando

"Sure he would," interrupted Antonio.

Rolando evaluated his uncle. "How would you do that? He is much bigger than a chicken."

"Rolando, I have a big gun I brought from Italy." Sal nodded toward the house.

"Would you have to kill him?" Rolando seemed upset.

"Unless you could convince him not to attack and I don't think he would listen to you." Sal said thinking that if Bruno did attack that gun was far away.

"What would Bruno do?" Rolando asked.

"He'd attack the chickens and anyone who was in the yard. I can tell you he wouldn't eat the vegetables and the fruits are pretty safe."

"Tino could protect us." Rolando looked at the small dog tied to a stake next to his house.

"Tino?" Antonio spoke out. "Bruno would eat him in one bite. No, we have to kill him."

Sal could see the consternation on Rolando's face. "Look, Bruno is tied up and the police have told the Crepiscus to keep the dog in the yard. Bruno lives in a big cage. He's trapped in there."

"A trap." Rolando smiled. "We could build a trap so when he came he'd fall into it. Then we could call his family and they would come to get him."

Sal only shook his head because they had not done the calculating that would maneuver a wild dog to just the right spot for a waiting trap. He did not want to discourage them. "That's it, Rolando, a trap. Now go off and play. I assume the chickens are fed?"

"Oh, yes, all fed and watered," Rolando said as the two ran off not to the woods, but to the tool shed. Normally, Sal would check on what they were doing, but today he was tired. He needed to finish the garden.

When Sal was finished and ready to see what Rolando and Antonio were doing, he remembered Roberto who, he hoped, was painting the garage. He gave Tino some water and a biscuit he had taken from the kitchen. He took time to talk to the animal to show him that he was loved. As he petted the grateful Tino, Sal took a deep gulp of water and looked up to the drifting clouds. A storm was coming. He walked back under the grape arbor that covered the walk from the garden to the house noticing that the wall had not been painted. He also noticed a large beautiful convertible parked in the driveway. It was Dominic who was staring at the garage.

"Boungiorno, Dominic," Sal called out but Dominic continued to look at the garage. It was only when Sal could see what Dominic saw that he also gazed. The roof had been painted in red, white, and green stripes and the rest was a desert scene with a crescent moon, a bright star, and a domed building. It was right out of the Arabian Nights. Sal realized he would have to repaint everything.

"How do you like it, Uncle Sal?" Roberto beamed with pride over his art. "I saw the picture in our Bible study book. It's Bethlehem when baby Jesus was born."

"And where is baby Jesus?" asked Dominic.

"He's in the house on the right with all the animals. You can't see him, but the star shows where he is. Do you like it?" Roberto was covered in splotches of paint as was Sal's hood of the car, which he had forgotten to move.

Before Dominic could answer, Sal said, "I should have been more specific as to how to paint it, but it is a beautiful job. Very creative. Right, Dominic?"

"It almost makes one religious," said Dominic.

"I thought of doing the Ark on the side. They had animals, too." Roberto said.

"No," Sal said. "It is enough for one day. It looks like rain and we want the paint to dry like it has on my car."

"It looks like your car has a rash," said Dominic.

"Talking of cars, is that yours?" Sal walked over to the convertible.

"It belongs to the boss. I was in the neighborhood so I thought I'd stop in to see if you needed anything at the grocery. I thought maybe Rosalina would like to come along and pick out what she needed." He glanced at Sal and it was obvious that it was more than shopping that he was after.

"Yes, a lot of groceries are needed to feed eight children. Perhaps Josephine and Francesca would like to go. I know Maria and Yolanda would. You see Rosalina comes as a package." Sal put his hands into his baggy pants.

Dominic sighed. "I understand, Sal. I only want Rosalina to be a friend, Okay? No complications. Just a good friend."

"Dominic, you are already our friend. When you came back after that meal I knew you were a friend."

Dominic looked down at his shoes then at Sal. "There's another reason."

"Oh?" Sal waited for the real reason of the visit.

"My parents are coming to America for awhile and I wanted them to see that I had friends who were...well...hard working people and not...well...weird artist types." Dominic shrugged.

"Uncle Sal, can I go now?" Roberto called out. "I put the paint away."

"And cleaned the brushes?" Sal thought they had their own weird artist.

"With soap and water."

"But it's an oil base paint and..." Sal knew the brushes were destroyed. "Thank you."

"I shouldn't have done that with the brushes, right?" Roberto said already knowing the answer.

Sal waved him off. "It's fine, Roberto. I'll just steal a few more next Tuesday." They all stared at him. "It's a joke," Sal said his hands opening in a 'do I have to tell you everything'. Roberto ran off. Sal turned back to Dominic. "When are your people coming? Why are they?"

"They ran into a little problem back in Sicily. Money was borrowed from the syndicate to cover bank costs and the money is slow coming back. The syndicate thinks there is some fast dealing by my father and now wants all their money. If he comes to America for awhile, by the time they figure where he is, the money will be in and so everything will be fine." Dominic said, not confident in what he had said.

"Syndicate? You mean..."

"Si," Dominic cut him off. They both knew he meant Cosa Nosta.

"They're dangerous to deal with," Sal said.

"But sometimes very necessary."

"So we become a cover, eh?" Sal shook his head. "Why us?"

"I hope not. I hope it is soon over like a big storm that is coming, then clear skies." Dominic looked at the bank of dark clouds in the west.

Rosalina, Yolanda, Maria, Josephine, and Francesca were staring out the second floor window at Roberto's art. Sal could see Francesca pointing but couldn't hear her. Then they all disappeared from the window and reappeared on the stairs.

Dominic noticed them and said, "I've never seen the rest of your house. How many bedrooms do you have?"

Sal answered mechanically as he watched the girls come down the stairs, "Two in the basement, two on the second floor and four on the third floor."

"Sal," Rosalina finally spoke. "What is this?"

"It's the birth of Jesus. Roberto was inspired by a book he got from your church."

"That's where baby Jesus lives." Francesca pointed to the lighted house.

"And that's the star," Josephine said. "Where are the three wise men?" Sal was impressed with her knowledge.

"There they are," Yolanda said pointing at the corner of the garage to the right, but there were only two kings. Yolanda went to the edge and looked at the far side. "Here's the other wise man, the angels, the shepherds and more stars."

Rosalina evaluated the garage looking at Sal then Dominic. "Do you like this, eh?"

Sal hesitated. "At least it's painted. It won't get rot. What's the harm?"

Yolanda objected. "I just wish Roberto would have told me. I could have helped."

"Me too," added Josephine.

"He's planning to paint Moses and the Ark on this side," said Sal.

"You mean Noah. Moses is the ten commandments," said Dominic.

"Oh, so the one who doesn't go to church knows about Noah," Rosalina said smiling at the guest. "And why are you here today? Have you become an art critic as well as a chef?"

"No, just the driver of this beautiful convertible who wants to take you, and whoever you want, to go with you shopping."

Rosalina squinted at him then looked at Sal. "Shopping? Who said I needed to shop?"

"With eight hungry kids and a man who wants to cook, you always need to go shopping. Right?"

Rosalina continued to look at Sal, "Did you put him up to this?"

Sal walked over to Rosalina. "Dominic just wants to be a friend. Understand? His people are coming to America from Sicily and he wants to show off." Sal turned to Dominic. "Isn't that right?"

"Right," Dominic said.

"Rosalina, if you don't go, I'll have to go and I'm tired," said Sal.

"Okay, for your sake, Sal, I'll go shopping but I'm taking Francesca and Josephine. Then let's go. I want to be back before the storm." She turned to Sal. "I'll need some money."

"Don't worry about it," said Dominic. "I'll take care of everything."

Rosalina abruptly turned to stare at Dominic. "You'll take care of everything?"

"Sorry, I just want to be a friend." Dominic in his enthusiasm had crossed a line.

As Sal gave his sister some money, she asked him, "Why are his people coming to America?"

"I'll explain later. Just remember to buy three big paint brushes for the Ark. There are a lot of animals to paint."

Chapter 10

After Dominic left, Sal studied the garage taking in the idea of a baby Jesus. He thought about his early years when he had gone to Mass, been confirmed, prayed to the saints, and believed in the Pope. It had been comforting to belong to something large, to enjoy the music, to be part of the history and its way of life. Now in support of his sister who had turned against the church since the death of her daughter, he was by necessity becoming a Pentecostal. The contrast was striking. They seldom talked about the death of Jesus, but more about being filled with the Holy Spirit. They did not have set prayers, but they sang and cried a lot. Sal figured that if he supported his sister and the kids with affection, everything would turn out fine. God would understand. That's what he did best.

"So you like it that much?" Yolanda came up to him carrying Sam. "Wait till you see my painting of Noah."

"It certainly gets your attention." Sal watched Sam eat a biscotti. "Not too much sweet, okay?" It was then he noticed how dark it had become. "Rain, and soon. I'd better hurry to get the basil for the pesto." He leaned over and gave Sam a kiss on the cheek but looked at Yolanda. "When are we going to meet this Marcello?"

"Tomorrow. He really wants to help."

"His father isn't in construction. Where did he learn to lay brick, or build a wall?"

"Well...ah...I don't know if he can, but he knows how to use a wheelbarrow. It's a start, right?" Yolanda grinned sheepishly.

Sal thought that a monkey could do as well. "Yes, it is a start. He'll be fine if he's willing to learn, but he'd better be willing to learn. If I see he's doing this just to get to you, he's out, understand? Capise?"

"Yes, Uncle Sal. You'd better get that basil." Yolanda looked at one of the kindest men she had ever met. "Josephine wanted to make some, too. Will you show her?"

"Of course, but I would have thought you or her mom could do that."

"She likes your pesto," she said as Sal nodded and hurriedly left.

Upon returning with a large bowl of basil, Sal noticed the rain beginning with large pellets, and a convertible racing up the driveway. As the car stopped, doors were flung open and Rosalina, carrying two bags of groceries and pushing two children dashed from the car. "Hurry, Rosalina, hurry, I have to get the top up."

"Okay, okay." Rosalina said pushing the two girls in front of her. "Go." They ran past Sal as a panicked Dominic pushed every button on the dashboard. He could hear something whirl but the roof stayed down, and the rain increased. Sal then saw three boys run madly toward the house from some undisclosed location in the woods.

Sal grabbed Rolando and gave him the basil. "Put this near the sink," Rolando grabbed the herbs and kept running into a house that reeked of garlic. Sal moved toward Dominic. "What's wrong?"

"I don't know. The roof is stuck and the car will get drenched. My boss will kill me." It was now a torrential downpour.

"Dominic, come inside. It can't get any wetter than it is. I'll get a towel." He motioned for Dominic to follow him up the stairs so that he wouldn't be the center of attention. "Vienne qui."

Dominic pressed again and heard the same whirl. "Damn it. Every time I come here I run into a disaster."

"Dominic, don't force..." Sal was trying to yell over the thunder, but he couldn't be heard. Then he did hear the sickening rip of canvas as part of the roof came up, the other part being held firmly in place by the safety latch that Dominic forgot to move. The two only stared at each other in the rain. Dominic shrugged and walked slowly to the stairs and into a large room where he received a towel.

"I'll get some clothes for you while yours dry. Care for some coffee?" asked Sal.

Dominic slowly dried off looking about the room that could have been a dining area, then outside to a car which was becoming a pool. "Do you have Sambucca?"

"A little. Want some in your coffee?"

"Yes, but forget the coffee."

When Dominic came downstairs to the kitchen he expected to be the laughing stock of the family not just because of the car, but for Sal's baggy clothes. No one seemed to notice. "Wow," Dominic blurted out, his eyes watering from the intense smell of garlic. Despite the rain, several windows were open and some water was coming in. "What's happening?"

"Rolando fed the chickens with the bag of garlic pieces instead of feed," said Rosalina. "Now we don't have to put any garlic in." Rosalina evaluated Dominic finding him more human, more like a man instead of a model. "Did you get the top up?"

"Most of it," Dominic said not wanting to discuss the debacle. "May I help?"

"All of the vegetables need to be cut," Yolanda said holding a knife in front of a pile of onions, mushrooms, carrots, and celery." If you could help with these, I could make sure the kids were fine."

"It's the wrong knife and where is your cutting board?"

"Cutting board? We use the table." Yolanda handed him the knife.

Dominic put her knife away grabbing a larger one with a curved blade. "This one will do until I can get a chopper. You see with this curved blade it will rock back and forth, see?" Dominic demonstrated on the table.

"No, I don't see."

"Yolanda," Rosalina spoke, "please get Dominic my cutting board. It's on the top shelf of the sheet closet, wrapped in a dark cloth. It was a gift from the mayor of Cefalu for some work your grandmother did for the city." She smiled at Dominic. "As far as a chopper, we have one in the garage with all of the other things we don't use."

"Ah, yes," said Sal. "I remember it." Sal pictured the curved knife next to an assortment of other instruments that could have been Inquisitional. There were times Sal had to worry about Giorgio's judgment as to what constituted a payment. He was showing Josephine how to trim the basil and parsley so that it would grind easily.

Yolanda returned with one of the most attractive cutting boards Dominic had ever seen. It was made of serpentine marble with a silver handle. He studied the embossed enamel picture of a peasant woman in a kerchief carrying a basket of blood oranges. He placed the board on the table and began a display of rapid cutting few saw except the professionals. Everyone stopped what they were doing to watch the baggy pants chef go through the pile of vegetables in just over a minute, normally a fifteen minute task. When he was done he looked at his admirers. "I would have done it faster but I didn't have a chopper, and this blade is a bit dull."

The rain pelted the windows and the open car, but inside, as Dominic cooked, as the table was set, and as the cheese was being grated, Rosalina brought out the mandolin and played songs of ancient Sicily.

"I know that song, Rosalina," said Dominic as he began serenading the family in a soft tenor voice. Rosalina joined him, then Yolanda, then Sal. They sang of sunny Sicily and of honor and of love. They sang of a land they had to leave, but had not forgotten.

Even when the lights went out, the music stopped just long enough to get candles and a hurricane lamp. Everyone gathered around the table. The dinner was served in the amber glow of fire that reflected off the smiling faces. They sang, they ate, they joked and they poked. When the lights returned Rosalina told Yolanda to turn them off because they were happier in the candle light. At one point as torn bread was passed out to the family and dipped to get the last portion of pesto, Dominic looked across the table at Rosalina, and he liked what he saw. Rosalina noticed that look but did nothing as she talked to Roberto about what he was going to paint. Sal also noticed the exchange of glances as he cut pieces of provolone for the kids. He saw that the friendship was deepening, but was it deep enough to include eight children? He liked the idea of an extra hand around the house; especially a hand that knew how to cook. So much is fate, he thought. So much.

Chapter 11

"Why don't you show me the rest of your house? Maybe by then my clothes will be dry." Dominic asked Sal.

"It's a house. What is there to see except who did their laundry or cleaned their room?" Rosalina asked as she collected plates.

"There's plenty to see. Pictures or mementos. Who knows? Maybe the type of wallpaper." Dominic stood. "Or why badminton rackets are on the wall."

"Show him the chandelier," said Yolanda.

"And the mural of the garden," added Roberto.

"What about a tour of our bathrooms?" Sal asked looking at Antonio who looked away.

"Sal," Rosalina stopped working. "just show him the house so that the man can come back for some pastry."

At the basement level was the kitchen, the T.V. room, Sal's room, a small bathroom, and Antonio and Roberto's bedroom. The second level was comprised of Francesca and Josephine's room, a dining area that was not used, Rosalina and Sam's room, a larger bath, and a living room that displayed an inappropriately massive chandelier with eighty lights and three hundred and twenty crystals. The thing took most of a day to clean.

As they began going up the final stairs, Dominic noticed a large grandfather's clock of carved red cherry on the landing. The only problem was that it did not have the slow stately tick of a grandfather's clock. As a matter of fact it had the rapid tinny sound of a cheap alarm clock. And the time was off. And the pendulum did not move. When Dominic looked inside he saw the cheap clock resting at the base. Dominic turned to Sal for an explanation.

"It was broken several years ago. I won't go into detail but it involved one of the kids over winding it. It was such a beautiful piece that we decided to keep it for no other reason than for Giorgio's memory." Sal had a brief image of the tall mustached man who loved the children, Rosalina, suspenders and gathering junk. To this day Sal could not figure how that man could make so many deals while being a barber.

"Why not get it fixed? It's reparable." Dominic lifted one of the weights that would have kept the clock working.

"No one ever looks here for the time. Sure I can fix it, but it's not high on my list, but feel free to tinker. It can't hurt." Sal motioned for Dominic to move up the stairs.

The third level was where Yolanda and Maria shared a room, but Rolando had a very small room to himself. It was known as Rolando's cell. Dominic noticed it had only a bed, a bar for hanging clothes and was kept very neat. "That boy will be a monk," said Sal. "Or maybe a criminal, eh?" There was a large bathroom and one large room at the front of the house used as a play area when it rained.

"A lot of kids," said Dominic.

"And every one loved," added Sal.

The rest of the evening was spent eating pastry, playing some cards and just talking. The kids began sharing with Dominic some of their plans for the future. Yolanda wanted to go to school to learn art, Antonio and Roberto had their sights on the military; whereas Maria liked the stage. Josephine aimed at being a chef like Dominic, and Francesca, since she had just started school thought she'd like being a teacher. Rolando said only that he wanted to be happy. As they talked, Sal thought it was no harm in hoping, but life has a way of doing what it likes to those plans because so much of life is fate.

"And what of you, Rosalina?" asked Dominic noticing that the rain had stopped.

"My future, dear Dominic, is what you see around you. I want my children to be good, healthy, happy and grateful. When Samuel leaves, so do I." She took a sip of coffee looking at her guest with smiling eyes. "Life is a lot of work and it's always nice to have someone to help. Wouldn't you agree?"

Dominic knew exactly what she meant. "Sure. Sometimes I could use a helper in the kitchen. When Josephine gets older maybe she can help. She already does some cooking. She's over there right now making pesto, right?"

Sal only glanced in Josephine's direction. "She's a fast learner, but what about you, Dominic? What are your plans?"

"I want my own restaurant. With a little help from my parents... well..." He gave a furtive glance around the room. "You see I'm rather playful. I'm an artist. What I need is someone who can balance the books. You know, the business end but who can you trust today, eh? I make the money and they will steal it. I've got plenty of ideas so I need someone who can say 'no'."

"No!" exploded Rosalina as she stood. Dominic leaned away from her thinking she was addressing him until he noticed that Roberto and Antonio had dressed up Rolando in a dress. They had put make-up on his face so that he had red lips, rouge and big eyebrows.

"What are you doing?" Rosalina scowled at the three.

"It was a joke, Mama," said Antonio. "We were going to introduce Rolando as the ghost of Theresa. You know, to scare him, to get a laugh."

"A laugh?" Rosalina's eyes widened in anger.

"Rosalina," Sal spoke up softly. "Please let me talk to them."

"No!" She glared at her brother but talked to the boys. "Take off those clothes now and wipe off that face. It is not funny that Theresa died. No. Go." She waved them away from the room. The three fell over each other getting away from their mother's wrath. Rosalina remained standing, everyone silent. They all looked at each other not knowing what to say. Rosalina turned to Dominic. "Are you sure you want to be a friend to a family that laughs at death? Eh?"

Dominic wanted to tell her that a family that can truly laugh at death would be the very family he'd want but instead he said, "Rosalina, not to make fun at your daughter's death but you have to admit Rolando looked ridiculous. I've never lost a child or a parent or a friend or even a pet. I can only imagine that it must be terrible. I am so sorry for your loss. It is no laughing matter."

Rosalina nodded and sat down and slowly placed her head on the table and started to cry. Yolanda stood and went over to her mother. When Rosalina raised her head quickly everyone saw she was laughing not crying. They stared in disbelief. "Rolando looked like a fool. Ha! The ghost of Theresa. My God, if that's their idea of a girl, we have more problems then we thought." She looked around the table gently touching Yolanda's hand. "I know Theresa is gone but I have eight wonderful children, but..." She raised her voice so that the boys could hear her. "Sometimes they are very stupid." She shook her head. "Did you see the chest they put on her? She was Mama Lardo." She looked at Dominic and became serious. "Well here we are, Dominic. This is who we are." It was then she noticed his baggy clothes. "Can you imagine arriving to work at La Sprezza wearing that?" She pointed to his pants. "Maybe then you could ask for a raise."

Dominic looked at himself as did the others and he laughed as did the others. It was a laugh not just of humor but of relief.

When Dominic drove home past midnight in a saturated automobile he took Josephine's home-made pesto with him. It would be served as a welcome meal for his parents who were coming in two days from Palermo. They were to arrive at four in the morning to avoid any difficulties with the syndicate and be driven quickly to an apartment near Dominic rented by a fictitious couple— Mr. and Mrs. Bridges. In two weeks it would be over. He thought seriously of asking Sal to share some clothes so that no one could recognize them.

Chapter 12

Marcello was coming in the afternoon so Yolanda decided to take on the daunting task of cleaning the monstrous chandelier. She enlisted the aid of her three sisters. According to family history, the chandelier had been given to her great grandfather, Taddeo, by the church for repairs he had done on an organ. The chandelier had at one time belonged to a count but out of guilt for some misdeed, he had given the object to the church as a gift. There it stayed in the basement for years next to an oiled canvas that had some painting on the inside. The church, which did not know of the existence of either item until Taddeo discovered them while trying to get to the organ's support, was glad to be rid of them as payment. When Taddeo brought the chandelier home he saw that it was too large for any room, so it stayed in the tool shed with the canvas object. When Giorgio and Rosalina came to America and finally settled at li Picolo Giardini, the name they had given to their home, Rosalina's parents gave both objects to them as a house warming gift. The chandelier was put up, after the ceiling was reinforced, and the canvas with its picture was placed in a plastic bag and placed in the rafters of the garage, where it remained.

Yolanda was on the ladder removing each crystal from its elaborate hook. The crystal would be handed to Josephine who in turn gave it to Maria who would place it in a large pail for washing. Francesca would then take the cleaned item and place it on a towel for drying.

Roberto and Antonio, meanwhile, had found a small pellet rifle and a box of pellets hidden behind some wood in the garage so decided to do some target practice. Just as they were leaving the garage, Rolando came up. "Where are you going?" he asked. "Is that a gun? Where did you get a gun? Does it belong to Uncle Sal?"

"Will you be quiet?" Antonio said as he moved closer to Rolando to intimidate him. "We found it in the garage and we're going to the woods to practice. Don't tell Uncle Sal cause he'll find something for us to do."

Rolando looked at his older brothers suspecting something he could not put into words. "Then take me with you."

Roberto knew they were trapped. "Fine, just keep quiet." The three went in a circuitous route to avoid Uncle Sal who was in the garden. They skirted the doll house, went behind the chicken coop, hurried past the pear trees, then made a wild dash over a small open field in front of the beehives.

When they reached the woods with its small cleared area that housed several wood tables for eating out, they relaxed. They put up a shooting gallery of cans, toys, and bottles of varying sizes.

When they had shot what they had set up as targets, they told Rolando to get more things. As Rolando was looking, Antonio, impatient to shoot at something, shot at a bird. This opened the door to any living creature within sight. After hearing several shots, Rolando came back with an armful of objects and saw what his brothers were doing. He dropped his items. "What are you doing? Don't. Don't. They did nothing to you. Stop it."

"Shut up, Rolando. That's what hunters do," Antonio said, pushing Rolando away.

"That's what soldiers do," added Roberto.

"You're not soldiers and the birds are not your enemy. I'm going to tell..." Rolando burst into tears.

"Stop squealing like a little girl, "Roberto said "You don't even know how to shoot a gun. Try it." He handed the rifle to Rolando. "Go ahead, shoot it, sissy."

"I won't shoot animals."

"Of course not, deary," said Antonio, "but at least shoot it. There, shoot the baby doll. Go ahead. Shoot."

Rolando slowly took the gun from Roberto, then in a swift motion, using the gun as a bat, smashed it against a tree bending the barrel. He screamed "It's bad. No more killing animals. It's bad, bad, bad." He hit the tree repeatedly dislodging the trigger, and cracking the stock.

The two grabbed the gun from Rolando's clutching grip and threw him to the ground. When they saw the damage, Rolando became the new target. "So you like to smash things," Roberto said as he kicked his brother. Rolando let out a scream.

"Tie him to a tree," Antonio said picking up Rolando.

"Without his clothes," added Roberto. Rolando continued to scream for his Uncle Sal. When Antonio grabbed Rolando to put his hand over his mouth, the younger boy broke free. He ran a few steps and was brought down by Roberto who punched Rolando's arm. "Shut up."

Uncle Sal thought he had seen the three boys running to the woods, he thought he had heard some muffled cracking noises, but he knew he had heard a scream. Rolando's scream. Without any further thought Sal ran to the woods carrying his hoe dreading it was Bruno. What could he do against that beast with a hoe? He was going into battle unarmed against a ferocious adversary. He wanted his gun. He must be nuts, but he kept running. He heard another scream. It was Rolando, but where were his brothers? They were supposed to protect him.

He saw Rolando running from the woods followed by Antonio and Roberto. "I'm here, Rolando," Sal screamed. 'What is it? Is it Bruno?" He hoped he'd say 'No.' He saw Antonio roughly handle his brother and then Roberto carrying what looked like a gun. Sal kept running. They all looked up to see him. "What is it?" Sal repeated "What?" They were waving him back.

"No, Uncle Sal, no. Go back. Go back," they screamed at him.

It was then, when he had not yet seen his adversary that the ground gave way. Had he been attacked from behind? Sticks, grass, dirt and leaves flew about him, then he hit hard after about a six foot drop. Debris fell all about him. He lay there a moment wondering what had happened. Where was he? Was he injured?

"Uncle Sal, Uncle Sal." Voices, coming from above, sounded like the boys'. Was he dead? He looked up toward the voices and saw three faces staring down at him. He slowly stood up feeling for damage. "Are you okay? You fell into Bruno's trap."

What the hell was Bruno's trap? Then he remembered his conversation. He was bruised and cut but still in one piece. He wanted to scream but only said, "Is Bruno there? Are you okay?"

"Bruno's not here, Uncle Sal," said Antonio, "and we're fine."

"All of you? Even Rolando?"

"Ah, sure," Roberto hesitated.

"Except when they pushed me down when I broke their gun," said Rolando. "They were shooting the birds."

"Shooting the birds? With a gun?" Sal stood all the way, his eyes now nearly up to the rim. "Where did you get a gun? And could someone get a ladder, eh?"

Roberto ran off not only to get the ladder but to avoid answering the question leaving a stammering Antonio with his accuser and judge. "I...found... it in the garage behind some wood. It's a pellet gun."

"I know it's a pellet gun because I was the one who put it there for your birthday. He smiled at Antonio. "Happy birthday."

"Thank you, but it's broken." Antonio held up the broken rifle.

"Broken? Ah, yes, Rolando did it because you were shooting birds, right?" He nodded. "Good. Now I know what not to buy you. I was going to see how you handled this then perhaps you would get a twenty-two, then a shot gun. Now who knows? Maybe instead, I'll buy a kite."

Chapter 13

Marcello arrived early and not knowing that the basement entrance was really the main entrance went to the second level where the four girls were cleaning the chandelier.

Francesca answered the door and before her stood a tall blond stranger. "Hi."

"Hi. I'm Marcello. I'm a little early but..."

"Who is it, Francesca?" Yolanda yelled from the ladder. Maria looked up from her work and Josephine still held two crystals in her hand trying to give them to Yolanda. "Don't let any strangers in."

"It's a person named Marcello," Francesca said.

"Who?" Yolanda could not believe her ears.

"Marcello. He says he's early."

Yolanda felt compromised. She was in the middle of a messy job that had to be finished. "Did you say Marcello."

The young man came in. "Yes, Yolanda, it's Marcello. Why don't you..."

Seeing him walk into the room, Yolanda awkwardly stepped off the ladder into the bucket of soap which, in surprising her, she kicked. The bucket and its contents of dirty water shot across the floor spraying the three at the door. In falling backward, Yolanda grabbed what she thought would be a support—the curtains. They weren't a support. Down went Yolanda and the curtains. Maria stood there mouth agape observing the fracas still holding two crystals. She put them on the buffet that had a vase of large fake flowers and that's where the crystals would remain.

"What is going on up there? Mama yelled from downstairs directly beneath them. "Do you hear me? If I have to come up there you'll be sorry. Your Uncle Sal is bleeding. He has cuts and bruises all over him and Antonio and Roberto are in their room saying something about not joining the army. I have no idea where Rolando is. Now what happened?"

Yolanda stood up, her dignity more hurt than her body, and stared at a dripping Marcello. Maria ran to the stairs and yelled down, "Mama, Marcello is here and Yolanda fell on her rear. There is water everywhere.

At first there was silence from downstairs. "Maria, what's happening?" There was more silence. "Okay, I can see the water dripping through the ceiling. Everybody come down now."

Yolanda spread her arms. "What can I say? I was working on the chandelier and it's a big job. Welcome to my house, Marcello. Do you need a towel? Of course you need a towel. What's wrong with me? For me, I used the curtains."

Marcello looked at the mess in the room and started to laugh. "Yes, I need a towel."

After getting towels for everyone, they went downstairs drying off where they were greeted by Mama. "Your poor uncle fell in a hole and is all banged up, so, be quiet, please. He has to work in two days."

"Mama, this is Marcello. Marcello, my mother," said Yolanda as she reached the bottom of the stairs.

"Marcello with no last name?" She turned and said to Maria, "Make some popadillo for your sisters. She then knocked on the door to her left. "Antonio, Roberto, come out to meet Marcello. Then you can go back to your room and play Mussolini."

"My name is Marcello Bacci, Mrs. Raphaeli. My people own the Tivoli, the grocery store with the bocce court in the back. That's us," said Marcello.

Mama raised her eyebrows as she looked to the right where Uncle Sal was resting. The room was dark with only a small candle on top of the dark wood bureau. There was soft music and the place smelled of a barber shop. Next to the bureau on a sofa covered by a green cloth reclined Uncle Sal sipping a glass of something clear with ice.

Marcello leaned toward Yolanda. "Is he going to die?"

Mama overheard him. "No, Marcello Bacci, he is not going to die. Just then the two boys entered the room and Mama said, "Marcello, I want you to meet..."

"Keep them out of here, Rosalina. They can meet Marcello later. These two need to stay in their room, and no poppadillo for them."

Mama turned to the boys, "Well, you heard him." She turned to Marcello and spoke softly. "The one on the left is Antonio, on the right is Roberto." The boys only waved in recognition.

Marcello smiled. "I hear you like Mussolini."

Antonio stared at the guest. "I don't know. What does it taste like?" Rosalina waved them back to their room.

Sal sat up feeling every ache. "So you're Marcello. Your grocery store is in the building owned by Mr. Freeman. That's where I'm working in two days to make a wall." He took a sip of the clear liquid and rubbed his arm. "How I'm going to do that, I don't know."

"Maybe I can help," Marcello said.

"Oh? Tell me, how many wheelbarrows does it take to make a wall?" Marcello looked depressed. "It's fine, Marcello. I'm just in pain. You can be a big help. I'll show you how to mix mud, then you can bring it to me and I'll do the rest."

"Mud?" Marcello looked confused.

Yolanda spoke up. "It's what they call wet cement. For my part, I'll make some lunch and bring it to you and Uncle Sal."

"You seem to have everything figured out," said Mama. "Perhaps maybe you've already spent the money?"

"Speaking of money, how much do you charge for unskilled labor?" Sal asked.

"Charge?" Marcello looked at Yolanda then Mama. "It's free. There is no charge."

"Then I don't want your help."

"But why?"

"Because that is what you are worth, nothing. I pay minimum wage but after you learn how to make mud it's a half more. When you learn to put the mud in the right place, it's double minimum. Agreed?"

"Oh...well...sure. Do you deduct for lunch?" Marcello grinned.

"If I did that, you'd owe us money." Sal looked at Rosalina. "I need to rest. If you find Rolando, send him in." He looked back to Marcello. "Please stay for dinner. I made pesto."

"So did I," said Josephine, "but our friend Dominic took it for his Mama and Poppa who are coming from Italy."

"Are you from Italy?" asked Francesca.

"Not me but my parents are."

"Where in Italy?" asked Mama.

"My father's from a little town called Taranto. It's in the..."

"Heel of Italy," completed Sal, "and it's not so little. There's a naval base there with a beautiful harbor."

"One day I'd like to see it," Marcello said.

"So would I," said Yolanda. "I'd really like to see Sicily."

"Yolanda, it is a place you'd never forget," Sal said closing his eyes.

Chapter 14

"And where are you going so early in the morning?" asked Mama, of Antonio and Roberto. Everyone else was finishing their breakfast of egg-inside-toast.

"We have to clean Mr. Rudolfo's boat. He's the one who gave us the eels," said Antonio.

"You have to work for that mess?" Mama said drinking her coffee. Sal was already in the field hard at work. "And what about the garage?" she looked at Roberto.

"Yolanda said she wanted to finish it," Roberto said looking at Yolanda for reassurance.

"Yes, Mama, I promised I would finish the garage," said Yolanda visualizing large storm waves splashing against a tossing ark.

"Oh, so I'm going to do the cooking, the shopping, the laundry and, may I remind you, of the mess a certain person made in the chandelier room? I was hoping to go to church to help give out groceries, but I suppose that the poor can wait."

"Mama, "Yolanda turned to face her, "we are the poor."

"We are not poor, we are not poor, Yolanda. We just don't have money. I'm talking about the real poor, and besides, what about Samuel? Eh?"

"Mama, it's fine. Everything will get done. I want you to go to church. Any inside we can get with God is a good thing." Yolanda raised her eyebrows in a 'You know what I mean' expression. "Right now I have to do the dishes."

Mama turned to the boys who were waiting at the door nudging each other. "Okay, go, but be back before lunch. I don't want you slaving over eels. Maybe for a bushel of crabs that we can put in the spaghetti, but eels? No." She lifted her head quickly in a 'go' order.

"I can fix the curtain and work on the chandelier," said Maria. "Then I can help watch Samuel."

Mama was suspicious of Maria volunteering to do any work. "And?"

"And what, Mama?" Maria's eyes softened.

"What do you want?" asked Mama.

"Well, it would be nice if you stopped by Felizia's bakery on your way home and..."

"Buy you some cassata, right?" finished Mama.

"That would be nice," Maria said with a smile.

"For cassata, which is expensive, you must help me with the garage sale."

All the kids looked up, but Yolanda asked "What garage sale?"

"The one were going to have in one week. All that junk must be worth something and besides, we need to empty the garage. Who knows, we may actually put our car in there."

Maria looked down at a place that once held a plate. "Clearing that garage will be a full time effort." She thought, 'Why do I get the facts after I make a decision? Then again, there's opportunity for more cassata.'

"Francesca and Josephine, you will come with me to church unless you have other plans." Mama looked at each of the girls.

"I'll go, "said Francesca. She liked the church.

"I'd rather stay here and really clean the kitchen. We need olive oil," Josephine said.

"There's plenty of oil in the pantry in Uncle Sal's room," Mama said.

"Oh, I didn't know it was there, so I used the other oil to make my pesto. Can I please stay and clean the kitchen?"

Mama thought about 'the other oil', and could only think of the grape seed, but that also was in Sal's room, "What other oil did you use?"

Rolando stood up "I'm going to visit my friend near the spring in the woods." He stated the unusual fact as if it were the most usual thing to say.

"Friend, what friend?" asked Mama.

"His name is Gabe, and he lives on the other side of the woods. He likes to feed the animals like me." Rolando started to go out.

"Rolando," Mama said. "I have a few questions to ask."

Rolando turned "You mean about Gabe?"

"Yes, about Gabe. How do you know he's going to be there, eh?"

Rolando looked confused. "He's always there early in the morning like now."

"And if you don't show up, like when you go to school?" Yolanda asked, continuing to clean the dishes and without ordering Maria she gave her a towel to help dry.

"We only meet in the summer. He goes to some school but I think it's Catholic."

"Why don't you invite him for dinner, so that all of us can meet him?" asked Mama.

"He'll have to ask his mom and dad, but that's a good idea. Oh, do we have any biscotti? Gabe likes biscotti and pizzelles." Rolando asked.

"Oh just like you," Mama observed.

"Yes, we like a lot of things together."

"Could you describe him?" asked Mama.

"Sure, he's a lot like me except he's in the school band and he wears glasses. He likes the color green a lot." Rolando was thinking, moving his eyes about as if picturing Gabe in front of him.

"In the band?" Yolanda asked putting away the plates. "What instrument does he play?"

"A horn that's curved. It's about this big." Rolando spread out his hands to show an object that would be about eighteen inches across. "And it sounds beautiful, like a hum."

Yolanda turned to face her brother, "You've actually heard and seen this horn?"

Mama touched Yolanda on the arm. "Will you get Rolando four biscotti. Two for him and two for his friend Gabe."

Yolanda looked confused, but she did as she was told, giving them to Rolando who thanked her and ran out.

Yolanda turned to her mother. "You know this Gabe could be imaginary."

"We all need a friend, Yolanda, whether that friend is imaginary or not. What harm is being done? You have Marcello, Sal has his garden, Maria has her food, and Antonio and Roberto have each other, and Rolando has Gabe."

"I have Tino," said Francesca.

"Yes of course, Francesca has Tino," added Mama.

"What do I have, Mama?" asked Josephine.

"You are a good friend of the Kitchen."

"And you, Mama," asked Yolanda, "who do you have?"

83

"You need to ask?" Mama looked up toward the sky. "I have him, Yolanda. He is my best friend. It took a great deal to find him, but he's always there. Believe me, people come and go, but not him."

Yolanda thought, 'For my mother, God is the reason for everything. I wonder why and will I be that way?'

Chapter 15

Antonio and Roberto did not show up for lunch. Mama and the girls had made a pizza with all the leftovers they could find in the refrigerator. Pizzas at the Raphaeli's were always square with thick crusts. They managed to find artichoke, avocado, black olives, mushroom, and chicken. Uncle Sal came in just as the pizza came out of the oven. Having walked past Noah and the ark, and the end of the world, he was ready to eat. When he received a large square slice of the pizza he stared down at eggs that stared back at him. "Eggs? You put eggs in the pizza?" That's when he noticed strange curved pieces next to the eggs. "Ah yes of course, squid heads. This is going to be a great pizza." He looked up at the girls. "I bet you made this, didn't you?"

Each one of them nodded, grateful for his gratitude. "Guess what I put in?" asked Francesca.

"Is it found anywhere in the kitchen?" Sal asked with a smile, fearful she would say no.

"Yes, it's in that box." She pointed to a container with a red top.

"But that's the biscottis," Sal said.

"Yep, you guessed right." Francesca loved biscotti.

"And what about you, Josephine?" asked Sal.

"Sal," Rosalina said "just eat it. They worked hard for you."

"But biscotti?" Sal sighed. "Well there is plenty of oregano. I can smell it, along with cinnamon."

"Cinnamon? Who put cinnamon in the pizza?" Rosalina said with surprise.

"Just kidding, Rosalina." Sal bit off a piece of this homemade Sicilian delight that had anchovy, tuna, corn, and something green. Sal figured it was the last of his pesto. "Oh, that reminds me, where's Josephine's pesto? I never had any."

"Neither did I," added Yolanda.

Rosalina thought a moment. "No one had any. It all went to Dominic."

As they were eating, the phone rang which was unusual. Mama looked up to the wall phone, wondering who could be calling, this was pranzo. You shouldn't be disturbed at lunch.

"I got it," Yolanda got up. "It could be 'you know who'." She picked up the receiver.

"Who's you know who?" asked Maria. Mama whispered 'Marcello'.

"Oh?" There was a pause "Oh my." Yolanda looked upset. "Okay, yes just a moment, I'll get him." Yolanda pointed to Uncle Sal. "Dominic and his parents are very sick. They are going to the hospital. He wants to talk to you."

Sal looked at Rosalina and stood up. He grabbed the phone from Yolanda. "This is me. What's wrong? Sick? When? After eating the pesto? Dominic, what happened?

Diarrhea? Oh, violent diarrhea? You say its food poisoning? Yes I'll be there, of course. Yes I'll sign the necessary papers." Sal put down the phone, wiping his mouth of sauce from the hanging towel.

"So? Are you going to tell us?" asked Mama.

Sal looked sternly at Josephine. "Josephine?"

"Yes Uncle Sal?"

"Did you make the pesto like I showed you? You see Mr. Dominic is sick and they think it could have been the pesto."

"Oh yes, I made it exactly as you said." Josephine's eyes widened, not believing she could be the cause of Dominic's pain.

Mama got up and went to the cupboard "Maybe not, Josephine." She reached up and withdrew a half-full bottle of castor oil. "You used this didn't you, when there was no olive oil, right?"

Josephine nodded "Yes, I told you I couldn't find the olive oil, so I figured that ..."

"Castor oil?" Sal interrupted. "Then they're not sick; they are getting cleaned out." He smiled. "That's a nice way to come to America."

"They're not sick?" asked Francesca who had been holding her breath.

"No. Now let me finish my pizza." He sat back down, took a bite of pizza and looked at Josephine. "Mr. Dominic will feel a lot better in a little while, but if you're going to be a chef you must use the right ingredients." Sal looked around the table. "Where are the boys?" Before anyone could answer he noticed a grinning Yolanda, who was stifling a laugh. "And what's so funny?"

"I was going to give some of that pesto to Marcello. You wouldn't have a worker tomorrow."

"So you think that's funny?" Sal shook his head. "I'm wounded and my only worker would have the craps. Yolanda, you have a strange sense of humor."

Rolando walked in. "I'm sorry about being late, but I can't tell time in the woods." He walked past the family, washed and sat down. "Pizza. I love pizza. But what is this?" He pulled out a tentacle.

"It's squid." Said Mama "If you don't like it put it aside. Someone will eat it. And how is your friend Gabe?"

Sal listened as he ate his pizza, thinking of how Dominic would like their creations. "Gabe? Who is Gabe?"

"He's my friend who goes to the spring in the woods. Today he taught me about chess. It's a very hard game."

"Gabe?" Sal repeated.

Rosalina spoke up "Sal, lets talk about this later. You have to see Dominic."

Sal was thinking, 'Gabe? I never heard of a Gabe, and the only spring in the woods was near a rise in the ground. The water comes out of the side of a small cliff, but to get there you need to go very near Bruno and he had not heard any barking'. When his thoughts returned to the family, they were talking about a garage sale. "Where are Antonio and Roberto?"

"They went to clean Rudolpho's boat as payment for the eels. Rosalina squinted at her brother "I told them to be back by lunch. This is what I get for being a little friendly."

"Do you know Minnick's number?" Sal asked.

"Always. I keep it pinned to my blouse, when I would get a sudden urge for artichokes. No I don't know that number," she concluded sarcastically.

"Rosalina I have to get to the hospital; I just hope they don't keep me there when they see what I look like. Anyway get the number, call Minnick, get Rudolpho's number and call him to find out if the boys are there, Okay? I really have to go." He turned to the girls. "It was a delicious pizza. Please save some for the boys. And Yolanda your artwork should be photographed and entered into a contest. Everyone should see that you're a good painter."

"They will Uncle Sal, at the garage sale," Yolanda said.

"Good," Sal said as he left. Just as he got into the car, he asked himself, 'What garage sale?'

Chapter 16

The Salutatis had not been admitted to the hospital so the three of them sat in the waiting room, then they sat in the bathroom, then they went back to the waiting room. The Italians could not understand the lack of concern by the hospital. In Italy health came first, then payment. Here, everything was insurance, even the diagnosis was by insurance. They had not even seen a nurse let alone a doctor. With each passing minute, the Salutatis grew angry with the hospital and very concerned that they had been poisoned. They had come to America to be unnoticed and now this.

When Sal told Dominic about the castor oil, the Salutatis kept asking to be sure they heard correctly. "We're not poisoned?" asked Antoinette Salutati. "So the syndicate did not get to us?"

Massimo shook his head and spoke in a whisper, "How do we know they didn't hire the little girl, eh?"

"No, no, just castor oil," Dominic said in Italian, though both his parents, Massimo and Antoinette understood English.

"Then we're not really poisoned?" said Massimo.

"That's right Papa." assured Dominic.

"Then let's get the hell out of here." His father insisted. "As far as I'm concerned one of the staff could be part of the plot. Avanti."

Dominic explained to Sal that he had planned to take off a few days, but because of the drenched car and his angry boss he decided to work extra hours. He was nervous about his parents staying at his house because it was possible for the syndicate to trace their location, but they knew nothing of the Raphaelis. He pressed Sal to take his parents for just a few days. It was a good place to hide, provided that the kids didn't kill them instead of the syndicate. He said that Sal owed him a favor because of the clothes, the car, and the pesto.

"They're planning some kind of garage sale," Sal said. "And where will they stay?"

"Upstairs, you know, the big room they use for games. Do you have an extra mattress? If not I can get one." Dominic said.

"Upstairs? Dominic, we don't have air conditioning like you. Are they willing to suffer like that?" Sal asked.

"Sal, do you have any idea of what the syndicate could do?" Dominic put his thumb to his cheek bone and flicked it outward. It was a Sicilian gesture that meant 'need I say more?'

Sal looked at the Salutatis thinking how these people were now exiled from their wealth by fate. Could they have imagined just two months ago that they would be here in a foreign country fearing for their health and safety, confused that all their protections quickly dissolved? "Are you sure they will want to come to our house? It's a big step back from what they are used to." Sal whispered to Dominic.

"Let me ask them." He sat down next to his parents. "Mom and Dad, here's what we can do. You can stay at Mr. Pasquali's house which has no air conditioning, eight children, and who are planning a garage sale or you can stay at a comfortable hotel where you can easily be traced by the syndicate. At the hotel you will be left alone, but at Pasquali's house you will never be alone."

The two sat quietly waiting for another option and evaluating the two given. No words were spoken, only glances at each other then at their son. Finally, Antoinette asked, "What is a garage sale?"

"It's where we put up for sale all the junk we don't want hoping someone will buy it," Sal said.

"It sounds like it might be a challenge," Antoinette said, her husband staring at her in disbelief. "Perhaps I could help?"

"Help is something we never turn down," Sal nodded.

"I won't help," Massimo spoke, "unless I get a commission."

"Commission?" Dominic blurted out. "These people are willing to protect and feed you and you want to take what little they make to raise a family? Papa, they have eight children to take of. Their home has almost no furniture and this man slaves in a garden or sweats at odd jobs getting paid practically nothing. He gets no rewards in this life and look at the way he dresses. He has scratches all over him and he can't even afford to go to a doctor. And you want a commission."

"I hadn't really realized how bad things were until you pointed them out," Sal said. "However, I'm not so poor that I can't afford to pay a person who works for me. How much?"

"Fifteen percent," Massimo said with a smile.

Antoinette quickly stood up backing away from her husband. "So help me, Massimo, if you take that commission you can find your own place to stay and good luck. You and your schemes. Look where it has gotten you." Her voice grew louder. "Well? Look around you. Do you see any orange blossoms, eh? Because of your schemes we are not in our beautiful home in Sicily, but in a country that doesn't even have health care. I've been poisoned and we running for our lives. Look at my hair. It is a shambles. And my dress has vomit on it—my vomit. Massimo, look outside. Do you see grapes or olives or figs or palm trees, eh?"

Massimo studied his wife as she ranted noticing that some people had gathered to see what was happening. "Antoinette, we are gathering attention. We don't want publicity." He turned to Sal. "Okay, no commission, now let's get out of here."

"I insist that you take something for your efforts," Sal said.

"What can I say?" Massimo looked at his wife and the crowd that included a nurse.

"You insist?" asked Antoinette looking at Sal.

"Yes."

"Then the commission will be…" She picked a penny from her purse. "What do you call this coin?"

"A penny," Dominic said.

"A pinni? Okay. This is your commission. One pinni a day and no more." She looked at her husband than at Sal. "Agree?" Both men nodded.

"I think," the nurse broke into the conversation, 'that whatever was bothering you has passed. If you want to go home, you can, just settle your account with the cashier."

"You charged for this?" Massimo objected. "For what? I drive myself to the hospital, I sit in a room where the people are herded together like cattle, and for two hours, while I throw up, I don't see a doctor or a nurse. I'm not even given the courtesy of a glass of water. All you did was to get enough information so that you can bill me. What charge? We wouldn't treat animals this way. Is this the way you treat visitors to your country?" Massimo spoke with a strong accent and some of what he said was not understood. What was understood was his disgust as several people encouraged him with their comments and grunts.

Throughout the tirade the nurse remained unshaken. "No, sometimes we gun them down in our streets." There was anger in her voice and eyes. "Welcome to America, now pay." She walked away.

"I won't pay," said Massimo. He turned to his wife. "Let's get out of here."

As they were leaving, Sal excused himself and out of curiosity went to see what the charges were. He was told fifteen hundred and twenty-six dollars and asked how he wanted to pay. His reply, 'Do you accept pesto as payment?' only brought a confused look. Sal wondered what they would have charged had they done anything.

Chapter 17

Upon returning home, Sal was greeted by an acidic smell in the kitchen. Rosalina was at the stove near a steaming large pot whose lid was held in place by some string. "What are you cooking?"

"Crabs. Antonio and Roberto brought home a large basket from Rudolpho. That's why they didn't come home for lunch. They were crapping. Have you seen these things? They're ugly and they bite."

"Mama, that's crabbing," corrected Yolanda who was seated at the table doing some sketching.

"Okay, crabbing. Anyway, I had to boil water with vinegar and spice, then put them in while they were still alive. That's when Rolando and Francesca ran out of the room."

"Yeah," chimed in Antonio. "Boy the crabs jumped around the pot trying to get out. We had to tie it down."

Sal ignored Antonio's joy over the execution of his catch. "Crabbing? How is that done?"

The boys took turns explaining how they tied chicken necks with string as bait, how they threw the bait out tying the other end to the boat and waiting for the crabs. When the crab started to eat the bait and tried to take the bait, the string would pull away from the boat. Then they would slowly pull the string up until they saw the crab where it would be scooped out of the water with a large metal net on a pole and placed in a basket.

"You did this all morning?" Sal still had some difficulty picturing the process.

"Yeah," Roberto said. "It was boring sometimes, but at others, you couldn't keep up with the crabs."

"What did you eat all day?" Sal asked.

"Oh, Rudolpho said it wasn't good to eat while working but he gave us some crackers and water," Antonio said proudly having endured a Spartan morning. "Sometimes, men have to do without those things to get the job done."

Yolanda looked up from her drawing thinking about what was just said. She knew it was important, but didn't know why. She also wondered about what women had to endure, especially in having a child. She looked across the table to her mother. 'She had nine.'

"How did you go to the bathroom?" Sal asked, not liking the smell of the crabs. It was too barbaric this whole operation. It wasn't like fishing or going after squid or octopus. Even how they were cooked was rough and he wondered if eating them was going to be rough.

"We just went off the side of the boat," Roberto said.

Maria looked up. "You went into the same water that you got the crabs? That is disgusting." Maria screwed her face into disapproval.

Sal decided to change the topic. "Rosalina?" She turned to him. "We may have visitors for awhile. Dominic's parents, who were not totally pleased with our pesto, need to stay here for a few days; Mrs. Salutati said she could help with the garage sale."

Everyone became silent waiting for Mama's response. They never had anyone stay at the house. "The Salutatis? How many are there? Do they have children? You know they're welcome, but are they aware that we don't have the luxuries they are used to?" She slowly undid the twine that held on the lid waiting for a reaction from the pot.

"Where are they going to sleep? Not my room," Antonio objected.

"I figure the big room on the third floor." Sal was beginning to question the wisdom of having the Salutatis.

"Not much privacy," Yolanda observed. "And there will be more laundry and cleaning."

Rosalina took off the top and looked in. "They're all red."

"Then they're ready. Rudopho said red is ready." Antonio sat up in anticipation.

Rosalina looked at Sal. "Of course they are welcome, Sal. We don't throw strangers to the wild."

Crabs to the Raphaelis were a new experience. Rosalina had had crabs only once in her life and the crabs she had eaten were very different from the ones in the pot. The rest of the family had never tasted crab. "You have to peel them," said Mama. "Well, break them apart, then dig out the meat." Josephine frowned while Rolando looked confused. "There is some effort but they are delicious." Mama pulled out a large steaming crab as the others watched and put it on a plate. "Get some paper to put on the table."

"What kind of paper?" asked Yolanda.

"Shopping bags. Cut them up and cover the table. That way when we are done all we have to do is roll up the paper and throw it away." Mama waited until it was done. They stared at the red creature in front of their mother.

"That is one ugly thing," Maria said staring at the object.

It smelled of garlic, thyme, and oregano. Mama broke off a claw, then each leg. She showed them how to crack the claw with a stone she had brought to the table. There was a pile of stones for all of them sitting on the edge of the sink. Everyone had wondered why the stones were there. She dug out the juicy meat and ate it.

Sal watched with interest this new ritual of food. "What does it taste like?" he asked. Mama dug out some more and handed it to him. There was a strict rule about eldest served first. Sal tasted not only the meat but also the 'mustard' of the crab. The kids waited for a reaction. He smiled and nodded. "Not bad. Is the claw the only part you eat?"

"No, Sal, just wait. It gets even better," Mama said, handing each one a leg so that they could break it and get a taste. As they ate she opened the shell by lifting it from behind. This act brought a gasp from Maria and dead silence from Rolando and Francesca.

"Well," Yolanda said. "if it wasn't dead, it's dead, now."

They all looked at the inside, but Roberto was particularly interested in the arrangement of the organs. "Do you eat all of this?" he said pointing at, then touching the bulge in the middle of the crab.

"No, Roberto. Here you have to be careful. You must not eat this part." She pointed to the central white mass then removed it with a scoop of her finger. "And not this." Again she pointed to a semi-circular white gill-like structure, then removed it. "These can make you sick. Once they are removed, the rest is good to eat." They continued to watch as she broke the crab in half with a single motion exposing the rich white meat of the inner crab. She gave some to Sal, then to each of the kids beginning with Yolanda. Rolando let his piece sit on the plate.

"This is really good," said Roberto.

"Yes, it is," Sal added.

Yolanda ate some, but only nodded; whereas Maria said it would taste better if it were mixed with mayonnaise or fried. After the initial introduction, each person was given their own crab to eat or not eat in any way they chose. Antonio attacked the crab with gusto like a storming army consuming the meat as he brought it out. Roberto studied, then ate. Yolanda used a fork eating each piece carefully. Maria made a sandwich with pickles and mayonnaise, while Josephine did everything her mom did.

Sal ate wondering if it was worth all the trouble. "You know if you were really hungry, you'd better have several dozen of these."

"Enjoy it Sal," said Mama. "It's a gift so be grateful. "Now, what were the names of these people who are coming to live with us?"

Chapter 18

The next day Sal went off with Marcello as Mama was getting ready to take Josephine and Francesca to church with her. Antonio and Roberto were told to work in the garden then help clear the garage by throwing out everything that no one would buy. As usual, Yolanda would cook, clean and watch Sam while Maria would do the laundry, fix the curtain and prepare the playroom for the guests. Rolando went to visit his friend then he would come back to take care of Tino, feed the chickens and, the worst job of all, clean out the coop.

Everyone was about their tasks with Mama getting ready to leave when they heard Rolando scream in the woods. They couldn't make out everything but the word Bruno was clear.

"It's Bruno," said Roberto. "He's attacking Rolando." He grabbed a hoe and ran forward to defend his brother.

Antonio heard the growls and barking and ran for the house because he knew that a hoe would be useless. Against such a beast, only a twelve-gage shotgun would do and he knew exactly where Uncle Sal hid one in his room. As he ran, he yelled to everyone, "Get inside. Now. Bruno is attacking."

"Oh, my God. Mio Dio. Presto, presto, Yolanda. Get the baby. Josephine, Francesca, get inside. The beast has come. Hurry. Hurry." The girls did not need any orders; they were running. After Mama had made sure they were safe in the house, she came out. "Where is Rolando?" At first it was to herself that she spoke, then aloud, "Roberto. Rolando."

In the distance she could hear the tinny voice of Tino, then Bruno's deep, angry growl. Rosalina visualized a fight of such injustice her eyes welled with tears. 'The poor, brave thing. Trying to defend us with his small teeth. Oh, my God, he is tied to his house and he can not escape. He must fight. Then fight bravely little one. Give us time.' Passing her in a blur raced Antonio with a gun. She was shocked at first, yelling, "Antonio, what are you doing?"

"Don't worry, Mama, I'm going to save my brother. That Bruno is dead." He turned with determination and ran from her to the battle. It was then that Antonio saw Roberto running toward him carrying a hoe and behind him an imposing, but limping mastiff dragging a chain attached to a broken stake.

"He's too big, Antonio. Rolando is up a tree and Tino, is dead. The bastard." Roberto threw aside the hoe as he went into the protection of the garage. Without hesitation, Antonio raised the gun and fired. The blast was deafening, the recoil devastating. Antonio was flung to the ground, his rifle thrown from him. He had missed, but Bruno, who had been barking and clawing at the garage door, was stunned by the noise. The large dog retreated a few steps, and then noticed the unprotected Antonio sprawled on the sidewalk.

Antonio ran up the stairs to the second floor, and Mama retreated to the basement. Bruno followed Antonio, but fear was a greater stimulus then anger. Just as Antonio closed the oak door, Bruno smashed into it shaking the room with the impact. "That had to hurt," Antonio said with a smile.

Mama, realizing that they were safe for the moment, turned to Yolanda. "Yolanda, call the police. That beast should be..."

"They're on their way, Mama. I called."

"The first day that your Uncle Sal goes to work, this has to happen." Rosalina put her hands on her hips. "And where is your Marcello when you need him? Typical of men. Off playing some game, eh?"

"Marcello is working." Yolanda felt defensive. "He would defend us."

"Oh? So where is he?" She raised both hands in the air in disgust. "And the gun is out there."

As Bruno barked at the house, the people inside could see Rolando race to the garage and was let in. After a short time, both Rolando and Roberto ran out toward the doll house. Rolando motioned for Roberto to hide on the side of the house. Then he screamed, "Here, Bruno, Bruno. Here, you big beast, come here. Here I am. Come and eat me."

Bruno heard his name then saw what had been his first target. He ran down the stairs and directly at Rolando who was standing in front of the doll house. When Rolando was sure that Bruno had seen him, he went inside. Just as Bruno came in the front door filling the space with his large frame, Rolando went out the back door and locked it. Bruno slowly turned around to get out, but Roberto had locked the other door. A cramped Bruno yelped then he did what he would do in his own small house, he lay down to lick his wound on his paw.

By the time the police arrived, everything was calm. Mama had discretely told Antonio to put away the gun since there was no reason to complicate the situation, but the police were curious about the shot gun blast of the painted camel on the garage. They found a wounded but alive Tino in his house with a piece of Bruno's fur next to him.

Bruno, tranquilized, was handed back to the Crepiscus with a stern warning that if the dog broke loose again, it would be shot and they would be heavily fined.

Sal and Marcello heard of the incident while they were preparing a new batch of cement, but as usual, the facts were jumbled. In the gossiped version, Rolando was almost killed and Rosalina was scratched. Sal told Marcello to do the best he could because he needed to get home. He'd make sure things were fine and return as soon as possible. Marcello also wanted to go, but Sal insisted that the job must be completed.

When Sal got home, it looked like nothing had happened. Rosalina told Sal how Rolando and Roberto had tricked Bruno, that the police were angry about the Romanians and that Antonio had fired his gun. "Where is Antonio?" Sal looked around with a stern expression.

"In his room. He has a very sore shoulder and scratches where he fell after he shot the gun."

"As if I don't have scratches. I want to talk to him." He moved to Antonio's room.

"Be easy, Salvatore. He meant well." Rosalina knew what Antonio had done was wrong.

As Sal walked past Roberto, he noticed that he was drawing a detailed anatomically correct rendering of a crab that looked more architectural than biological, but said nothing. Sal knocked on the door, then walked in.

Antonio was in bed and looked exhausted. "So, you fired my gun, today." It wasn't a question.

"Yes, and I missed." He looked dejected. "I should have killed him."

"Killed. It scared you, so you have a right to kill it, right?" Sal shook his head.

"What would you do?"

"Stay inside and let the police handle it."

"But I wanted to…"

"Take the law into your own hands." Sal took a deep breath. "Look, I understand that you want to defend the family, but they were already safe. Were you defending or were you trying to kill Bruno? Or perhaps you just wanted to shoot the gun? To hear the explosion? To feel the power? Eh? What was it?"

"I wanted to be the man when you were not here who would protect us. Is that wrong?" Antonio possessed a defiant pout.

"Not that, but to take something that belonged to me and to do with it something I wouldn't do, that is why I am angry, as you would be if I had taken your favorite lacrosse stick to scoop crabs. Think of that." Sal started to leave but turned back. "Wait. I have a deal. You want to shoot a gun, right?"

Antonio sat up at this. "Yes, but I don't have a gun."

"You will. Be patient. The police offer a course on how to care for and shoot a gun. It costs a bit, but I am willing to pay."

Antonio was paying full attention. "The police show people how to shoot?"

"Yes, and I want you to take the course and while you are doing that, we are going to the pound to get a small dog for you to raise."

"What is the pound?" Antonio asked.

"It's a place people bring unwanted or stray pets. It's like a prison, only worse because after awhile, if no one comes for a pet, they are killed."

"How?"

"Injection."

"Even if they are healthy and friendly?" Antonio looked confused. "Could such a thing be possible?"

"Oh, yes." Sal wanted to say more.

"It's like what they did to the Jews in the war."

"No, nothing like that." Sal squinted, realizing the conversation had gone far enough and did not want to stray from the point. "Anyway, take the course and keep the pet healthy. When you finish the course, I'll get you your own gun so that you don't have to sneak into my room. Capise? Agree?"

Antonio liked the idea of his own gun, but raising a pet was not his style. Perhaps he could tie it up near Tino, then after he got his gun, the dog would be accidentally lost.

"And..." Sal broke into his thoughts, "you keep the gun as long as the dog is around."

"What kind of gun?"

"A twenty-two."

"That's not a gun. You can't kill anything with that." Antonio blurted out not realizing he shot himself in the foot.

"That is exactly what I thought you'd say. Now it's my turn to think over my proposal. I need a coffee." Sal turned to leave.

"Okay, Uncle Sal, okay. I'll do what you said, but it's a lot of work for a small gun." Antonio sat back on the bed.

"It is, but if you handle things correctly, who knows where it may lead. Maybe you'll get your own cannon." Sal smiled. "Now go and tell Rolando, our one day hero, to clean the coop and throw it all in the trash. It smells out there."

By the time Sal got back to the job, Marcello, pressed to make a good impression, had built a brick wall three feet high. When completed the building would house a bathroom for those playing bocce and bocce, to the men of St. Gabriello parish, was just as important as soccer. Teams from across the state would compete once a year in a tournament in which the winning team, composed of four men, would receive a fully paid two week vacation to Italy. Only men could enter, the minimum age was fifty (though there were other considerations), the entrance fee was one thousand, and they had to be Italian. It was never meant to be politically correct. There were a few disgruntled comments but they were politely ignored and the plaintiffs were invited to have some sweet Italian sausage.

As Sal and Marcello worked together they talked of the wall, bocce, soccer, the family, Bruno, then whatever came up of interest. At the rate they worked, they'd be done by tomorrow, then the plumbers and electricians would do their job. Everything would be done long before the tournament.

Chapter 19

The Salutatis arrived with Dominic the next day. They were shown the large room for their private living and the bathroom they would share. Mama could see immediately that the Salutatis were accustomed to a more luxurious life style. Even the questions they asked indicated wealth: Who cleans the room? When is breakfast served? When is the phone to be installed? Where do you place the clothes that are going to the cleaners? How do you turn on the air conditioning?

Dominic gently explained to his parents the dire conditions in which they had to live until the crisis was over and then insisted that he wanted to personally take care of dinner that night to help them get used to things. "So tonight, Mom and Dad, I am going to make your favorite meal, Sicilian Capanata. I know it is a little warm for you so we will try to get ice as soon as possible." Rosalina remained quiet, her arms folded over her waist listening to apologies being made for a life she lived every day.

"Could I at least have a chair and a lamp so that I can read the paper?" Massimo looked with disdain at his prison assuming there would be a paper to read.

"I'll see what I can do, Mr. Salutati," Rosalina said forcing a smile with lips that would have preferred to say other things.

Antoinette moved closer to Rosalina. "I know this must be difficult for you as well. Could I help with this sale?" Then she added in a much lower tone, "Could we talk outside?" After she closed the door, she spoke again. "We know this is a strain. Massimo is not use to living..."

"So poor," Rosalina completed her thoughts.

"We have become spoiled living on other people's money. You see if we don't pay the syndicate their money they could be very unkind to us. We could lose everything we have worked for including the bank. It is a great deal of money. Massimo trusted people who have betrayed him and he is not young. He could lose more than a bank, Rosalina."

Rosalina studied the woman as she talked, trying to gauge her sincerity. "Will this syndicate hurt you physically?"

"Perhaps. They will try to convince us to pay, but we don't have five million dollars." Antoinette lowered her eyes.

"Five million dollars?" Rosalina raised her voice in shock.

"Please, Mrs. Raphaeli, I don't want him to hear."

"But five million. How did he ever..." She stopped and stood very straight. "My name is Rosalina, okay? Now, tell me what happened." Rosalina extended an open hand toward Antoinette inviting her to speak.

"It's a long story, but it amounts to the fact that a group of jealous bankers wanted to get rid of Massimo because he was so successful in what they thought was only their territory. They secretly formed a group and hired people as a front to borrow large sums of money at high interest rates. Massimo should have been suspicious but he let greed go to his head. All of these people would then default on their loans forcing Massimo to borrow from less reputable sources to cover his expenses to his good customers. He went to the syndicate who was in on the deal. Now the syndicate wants its money. We have tried everything to get the money, even promising to pay more interest, but nothing has helped. If Massimo seems peevish it is because he will most likely lose everything. There are reasons, but not excuses."

The two women just stared at each other; Rosalina could feel her honesty and she reached out and touched Antoinette on the arm. "First of all it's called a garage sale, and yes you can help. Maybe we'll make enough to pay off the syndicate with a little left over to build a pool, eh?" They smiled at first then Antoinette started to cry. "Come on, let's go see what the boys are digging out of the garage we could sell." Rosalina put her arm around Antoinette as they walked from the room.

Chapter 20

Dominic was in the kitchen that he had converted to a serious work area. Knives were set out according to use, spices were within easy reach as were bowls, various vegetables, and cooking pans. He had been talking to Yolanda and Josephine as Maria fed Sam. They all became quiet as the women entered. Rosalina looked about. "Where are Rolando and Francesca?" she asked.

Yolanda shrugged. "They should be in the garage."

Rosalina then turned to Dominic. "So you are going to teach my daughters how to cook, eh?" She then glanced at the girls. "I guess you are ready to go beyond my skills."

"That can never be, Rosalina," Dominic said. He wanted to say much more. He wanted to sing to her, to write poems to her, to tell her of his affections but there was a timidity of expression. There was a fear of saying the wrong thing, so he remained silent.

"Oh?" Rosalina said. "And just what does that mean?" She glanced at Antoinette and Yolanda hoping to get Dominic to say what he was reluctant to say.

"Only that I know the notes of the song, but you know the music. Only you know the real tastes of your family. You know your children and their ways." Again Dominic was on the verge of saying more but looked at his mother and remained quiet.

"Dominic, it's just a meal," said Rosalina. "Try to keep it simple. Simple foods for simple people. I don't want them to get used to foods I can't afford no matter how they are cooked or taste, okay?" She was about to leave when she noticed Maria giving something to Sam. "What are you feeding the baby?"

"Pepperoni," Maria said with a smile. "He likes it."

"Pepperoni?" Rosalina took a deep breath in frustration. "Maria, Samuel will be up all night crapping and screaming that his rear-end is burning and you will be there to help, understand?"

Maria's shoulders sagged. "Yes, Mama."

When the two women were outside, Antoinette said, "I think my son has taken an interest in you."

"When he takes an interest in eight children, I'll pay attention. An opera needs more than one voice, no matter how good the tenor is." She pointed to the garage which the boys were emptying.

"Oh, Mama, see what I found..." Roberto started to point to a canvas object.

"Aspetto. Wait. Where are Rolando and Francesca?"

Antonio pointed to the woods. "They went to the spring. Rolando said he wanted Francesca to meet his friend Gabe. He said he'd be right back."

Rosalina stared at the woods wondering what was really happening. She would talk to them when they got back. Turning to the boys she said, "Which side is the junk?"

Roberto pointed to the right. "Most of that stuff is broken but maybe somebody can fix it."

"What about that chair?" asked Antoinette.

"It's all ripped up," said Roberto.

Antoinette looked at Rosalina. "Could I have that for Massimo? It will give him a place to sit."

"Antonio and Roberto," said Rosalina, "take that chair to where the Salutatis are staying." Both boys evaluated the piece of junk, shrugged and picked it up. Within moments the two had bumped and scraped the old brown chair to the second floor. They dragged it across the dining area and through the chandelier room then up another stairs where Antonio smashed his finger.

Massimo greeted them. He was wearing shorts and a tee shirt. "Well, what is it?" His face was red from the heat.

"We brought you a chair," said Roberto.

"I didn't order any chair," he insisted.

"Your wife said it was for you," Roberto replied.

"I'd rather have some lemonade," he said looking past the boys for the waiter.

"It's the chair or nothing," said Antonio.

"If I take it, can I have lemonade?" He frowned as he stepped back to allow them in. The boys quickly slipped the ragged object to the side of the room and started to leave. "Remember the lemonade."

"I'll do what I can, sir," said Roberto.

Little did anyone realize until hours later that Rolando had used that very chair as a dumping spot for the chicken poop.

At first the odor brewing in the confines of the chair in the heat of the day was slight, giving the room an unflushed smell. Then it started to seep to the other rooms. The smell went unnoticed since everyone was busy but eventually it reached the kitchen where Dominic had just made a large pot of lemonade for everyone's use. As he worked, Dominic kept checking his food to be sure it was fresh. The influx of the odor was subtle so that those in the kitchen gradually got used to it.

It was when Mama came in to check on them that the odor became apparent. Something was very wrong. "Dominic, what are you cooking? It smells really bad in here. Yolanda, go see if all the toilets are flushed and for God's sake Dominic open a window."

"Rosalina, I have only used the best but whatever that smell is, it will spoil it. Maybe a sewer line is broken." Dominic put tops on all his preparations.

"What's in the large pot?" asked Rosalina.

"Lemonade. It's fresh. I made it for my father but it's for everyone." He lifted the top to show her, scooped out some for a glass and then put the lid back on. "Josephine, please take this to my father."

Rosalina took the glass from Josephine. "I'll do it. It will give me a chance to meet him." She sniffed the air. "It smells like chicken poop. How can that be?"

Antoinette came in and stopped at the door. "Oh, my, something is not right. I hope that's not the caponata." She looked at her son. "Have you made this dish for the restaurant?"

"No. I was trying it here first," Dominic said.

"My advice is to burn the recipe or have it accidentally fall into the hands of your competition."

"Mom, it is not coming from my caponata." Dominic was getting upset. "Every time I come to this house something goes wrong." He looked at Rosalina. "Well, not everything."

"Mama," Yolanda came back. "All the toilets are flushed but the smell gets stronger the higher you go. It seems to be coming from the Salutatis room."

"Did you knock?" asked Antoinette.

"No. I didn't want to disturb him but it was definitely coming from there."

Rosalina gave the glass of lemonade to Antoinette. "Here. Bring this to your husband and find out what is happening. If he is that upset, I don't want to go in there."

Massimo was sitting in his chair when Antoinette came in. Not only was the room stifling since the windows were closed, the odor was overpowering. "Massimo, this room smells terrible. What have you done? How can you sit in a room like this?"

He stared at her noticing the glass of lemonade. Sweat was running down his face in streams. "Is that for me?"

"Yes," she said. "Drink this while I open the windows."

"But what about the air conditioning?" he said taking a drink.

"What air conditioning, Massimo?"

He took a deep swallow of lemonade. "This is very good. Who made it?'

"Your son." Antoinette opened the large window and immediately there was a draft of air that seemed cool in comparison to the stagnant room. Antoinette kept sniffing the air eventually centering on the chair. "It's coming from your chair." She looked at her husband thinking the worst. "It's not you, is it?" She stepped back studying her husband. He looked beaten. "Massimo, let's go downstairs. It will do you good to walk in the shade of the arbor. We could use your help in pricing the items for sale. Come on. Avanti, mio caro."

Massimo finished the lemonade and looked at his wife. "It smells like shit in here, but I was afraid of going out. You know they may see me."

"Who may see you, Massimo?" She gently walked her husband to the door.

"The syndicate, that's who. If we stay hidden, we can escape just like we did when the Americans came to chase out Il Duce." Massimo's family support of Mussolini was a topic seldom discussed. That support had forced the Salutatis to move from Florence to Sicily and begin fresh.

The Salutatis met Rosalina in the chandelier room. With her were Roberto and Antonio. Antoinette said, "It's the chair, Rosalina. There is something in..."

"I know about the chair," Rosalina said. "I found out what Rolando did with the chicken poop. He thought the chair was part of the trash. Does it ever end?" She turned to the two boys. "Go, get that chair out of the room, open the windows and empty this into the room." She handed them a fragrant spray.

The boys went up the stairs making strange guttural noises and making comments comparing the smell to various people they knew. When they got to the room, they ran into another problem. "Are we going to drag this piece of crap through the house?" asked Antonio.

"What else can we do?" asked Roberto. They both stared at the large open window. "Will it fit?" Roberto knew it would.

It was then that Antonio noticed that the chair was smoldering. Massimo in his depressed state of mind had dropped his cigarette into the old chair with its exposed stuffing. It was on fire. "Hurry," said Antonio. "Get it out of here or the whole place will catch on fire." They got it to the window and through it. Their plan was to put it on the sloping roof, get outside with it, move it to the side and drop it safely to the yard. The chair did not cooperate. Being exposed to the fresh breeze, the chair erupted into flames. It fell from their grip, rolled down the roof to smash on the front stairs spraying flaming chicken poop into the front yard.

Antonio and Roberto were not the only ones to see the chair fall. Sal and Marcello had just reached the house when they witnessed a flaming chair roll out the third floor window and into the yard. "Look at that, Sal! My God!"

Marcello pointed to the chair his mouth open in shock to see small bits of sparks jump in all directions.

"Marcello, please," said Sal. "If you're going to get upset about a simple thing as a chair on fire being thrown out the window you'll never make it in this family."

The chair remained where it fell as a charred momento until the day of the sale. Dogs and cats would gather around it. It would be the same day Antonio would bring back from the pound a small Italian sheepdog he had named Enzo, after his grandfather.

Chapter 21

After a dinner in which fourteen people were served, Dominic, Josephine, and Yolanda glowed in the praise of a well prepared feast though periodically one could detect a residual odor of the chicken poop. During the meal Mama would occasionally remind Maria of being careful of how much she ate, and compliment each of the children for something they had done well during the day. Dominic had never done that, but why should he? He had always been single and his concern had always been for himself. He now began to see not only Rosalina in a different light; he was seeing the children differently as much as he was re-evaluating himself.

Massimo, lost in his thoughts, drank more wine than usual worrying about a dangerous future, but he smiled once in a while over a passing joke. Antoinette talked of her home in the Syracusan suburbs, Marcello talked of the brick toilet he was building, Sal wondered about this newly emptied garage, and through it all Sam ate, played with the food, farted and generally entertained the rest of the gathering.

When the meal was over and Dominic told Josephine that clearing the table and cleaning the dishes were part of being a cook, Yolanda decided she wanted to take a walk to see Marcello's job.

Mama thought about it for a moment knowing it was a twenty minute walk one way and most of that way would be dark. She was about to say no but read the plea in Yolanda's eyes. "It's a long way in the dark."

"Don't worry, Mrs. Raphaeli," Marcello said. "She'll be in good hands."

"That's what I was thinking about," Rosalina finally smiled. "Go, but don't be too long. You still have work to do." She hesitated then said, "Wait, Yolanda. Do you know how to play bocce?"

"I think so. You throw a little ball on the lawn then each team tries to get their larger balls close to it, right?" She looked around the room for some confirmation.

"So far so good," Mama said. "And how does one score?" There was a smirk of innuendo.

"When one of the men gets his balls very close to the little one, he wins." She looked at Marcello who nodded then at her mother who had a strange smile.

"And do you know what bocce means?" asked Mama.

"Of course. It means to kiss, eh?" Yolanda was beginning to worry about all these questions.

Rosalina's eyes softened to see her little girl, now seventeen, blossoming. She remembered being seventeen when she had been kissed by Franco, her first boyfriend. That kiss came on a night very much like tonight, but it was in Sicily, and it was one kiss. Soon after that, she met Giorgio and all her kisses were for him. She wondered what ever became of Franco. The last she heard he was living in the hills a little south of Cefalu in some sort of import business. Ah, fate. How can we take this life so seriously with fate?

"Mama?" Yolanda spoke loudly to get her attention.

"What?" Mama came out of her thoughts. "You don't have to yell. Are you still here? Go. Who knows, from the building of a toilet can come great things." She realized that she had just said a stupid thing but turned to Rolando. "Rolando, where is your sister, Francesca? I want to talk to both of you."

Rolando looked confused because his sister was sitting next to him. "Here, Mama."

"Yes, of course. Next time speak up. Come with me. I need to talk in private." They followed her upstairs to the dining area never used that overlooked the backyard. There was a small table in front of the window and several mismatched chairs. "Sit down." They quickly obeyed because she was acting unusual.

"Did we do something wrong, Mama?" asked Francesca.

"That is what I want to know. Who is this person in the woods?" She turned to Francesca. "Have you actually seen him?"

Francesca blinked. "Do you mean Gabe?"

"Yes, I mean Gabe. The one with the horns."

"Horns?" Francesca's eyes widened in horror. "I've never seen him with horns."

"I never told her about him being in the band, Mama," Rolando said.

Rosalina looked at Rolando, then at Francesca. "Tell me about him, and Rolando, keep quiet. And don't talk with your eyes."

"He looks like Rolando but a bit taller, he likes green, and he likes the animals like I do. Oh, his mother and father are vegetables, and Gabe likes to play games." She smiled waiting for approval.

"His mom and dad are vegetables?" Rosalina asked.

"You know, where you don't eat animals," Francesca said wondering what she had said wrong.

"Ah, of course, and what sort of games does Gabe like to play?" Rosalina feared the answer.

"I think it's called chess and another game with lots of triangles. You need dice for that game. I don't understand those games but Rolando plays."

Rosalina faced Rolando. "What do you talk about?"

Rolando thought a moment. "Trees, animals, why people get angry. We talk about our families and we talk sometimes about God."

"God?" Rosalina was surprised. "What about God? Does Gabe believe in God?'

"Very much. He says God is everywhere and that's why we shouldn't kill animals. I like Gabe. I'd like you to meet him."

"That is exactly what I want to do." Mama sat back in the chair.

"His mom and dad said he could come to our dinner after the operation.' Francesca said.

"Operation? What's wrong with him?"

"Not his operation," Rolando said, "his mom's operation. She has something wrong with her stomach, but she'll be fine. His dad wants him around the house in case he's needed so we won't be seeing Gabe for a while."

Mama looked at them. "So there really is a Gabe?"

Francesca and Rolando looked at each other confused about their mother's question but answered in unison, "Yes." Then Rolando added, "Do you think we were making him up?"

"It's been done before. I used to have a make-believe friend who was a mushroom. My mother made a huge mushroom out of a cushion from the sofa. It had a mouth, ears, nose, and very pretty eyes of blue. I would sit with

Mario, that was his name, and tell him all of my worries and he would just listen to me. He wouldn't tell me what to do but just by listening, I could figure things out. I thought maybe Gabe was like that."

"Mama, mushrooms can't talk," Rolando said wondering why his mother told them about her cushion friend.

"I know that. I was just saying that it's normal to have make-believe friends." She smiled hoping that her confession would free them to talk.

"Gabe isn't make-believe, Mama," said Francesca. "I know the difference between pretend and real." She was a little hurt at not being taken seriously.

"Good." Mama stood. "I wish I did. Our talk is over unless you have something to say or ask."

"Do you like Dominic?" Rolando asked.

The question stopped Rosalina in her movements. "Well...I...really haven't thought about it much. Yes, I like Dominic. Of course I like Dominic. I like the way he cooks and..."

"Are you going to marry him?" Francesca asked.

"First of all it's none of your business and secondly, he hasn't asked me." She straightened herself smoothing out her impossibly wrinkled dress. "For right now I want to meet Gabe as soon as possible, understand?" They only nodded and ran off. Rosalina stared after them. Dominic as a friend? Yes. Dominic as a lover? Maybe. Dominic as a provider? Why not? Dominic as a father? That is the question.

Chapter 22

Sal went outside to examine what was in each of the piles periodically looking at the shot gun blast in the garage. He told Antonio and Roberto to take a good chair up to Mr.Salutati as well as a lamp so that he could read. "Try to make the old man comfortable. He has seen a great deal of life and he probably wants to rest. If he wants some coffee, get it for him."

"What if he wants to talk? Old people like to talk," said Roberto.

"Then listen. Maybe you'll learn something. Being kind to him is for your sake as well as his." Sal realized the point was likely missed.

The two decided to take the chair to the front of the house where the steps were wider and less steep. They carried the chair past the burnt remains of the old one and with ease entered the house, went through the chandelier room and were going up the last stairs when Antonio said, "I can't figure Uncle Sal. How is doing all this work helping us?"

"It's a grown-up thing, Antonio. Let's get it there and get out, okay?"

Mr. Salutati was brushing his teeth when they knocked and let themselves in hoping no one would be there. "Ho," Massimo yelled after spitting the rinse from his mouth. "What have we here? A chair that is not on fire. And what sort of smell does this one have? Dog, hog, or cow?" He looked at the boys realizing his humor was too sarcastic. "Thank you for bringing the chair and lamp. I have few pleasures left in life: lemonade, listening to the madness of the news, reading a crime story, and if I were in Sicily, looking from my balcony to see the water. You know I live in Syracusa. It is a city with a great history. Do you know about Syracusa?" He reached over to the pitcher of lemonade and poured half a glass slowly dropping in three ice cubes. "I have extra glasses, would you care for some? My son made this with Sicilian lemons with a touch of blood orange that grows at its best on the slopes of Mt. Etna, the volcano."

All that Antonio wanted was to leave, but he remembered his uncle's words, stayed, and tried to be interested. "I've heard about Etna. It exploded a long time ago and buried a whole town that archeologists are digging up. They found a room where they were naked pictures on the wall." Roberto knew this was wrong but kept quiet.

"Wrong volcano, right idea. Volcanoes are dangerous. They are like certain people I know." He was thinking of Damio back in Sicily who went on a drive-by shooting spree of any dog because cats kept him up one night. For that he spent some time in the nut house, not because he killed the dogs, but because no one could make the connection between cats making out in the night and Senora Capelli's sick Chihuahua who hadn't made a sound in three years.

"Anyway, Syracusa was the home of great thinkers like Archimedes who almost single handedly defeated the Romans who were attacking the city."

This statement stirred some interest. "One man?" asked Roberto. "How?"

"By inventing clever machines that could burn the Roman ships with a beam of light or lift them out of the water, but there were too many Romans." He waved his hand in a dismissive manner. "That's always been Sicily's problem. They were invaded by the Greeks, the people from Carthage, the Romans, the Moors, the Normans, the Spanish and a whole lot of other people including the Americans. Everybody wants Sicily."

"What's there?" asked Antonio.

"Everything you'd need to live a good life if only people would leave you alone. What Sicily needs now is another Garibaldi or Mussolini. A mix of the two, but what do we have? The syndicate. The bastards." As the two boys looked at each other in surprise at the language, Massimo looked out the window to a landscape devoid of figs, oranges, grapes, the sea, mountains, palm trees and beautiful architecture. It was bland. What it did have was a large crescent moon on the horizon with a bright star. It was the same moon in Sicily and that somehow comforted the old man.

The boys waited in silence until Roberto, to break the sullen silence asked, "Who are the Moors?"

Massimo turned to face them. "The Moors." He motioned for them to look at the moon. "See that moon with a star? It is the symbol of the Moors. They were Moslems. They came out of Africa and brought with them science, spice, and song. There is one Moslem I like to quote. His name is Omar Khayyam. He said that the only thing worth while is wine. Everything else comes and goes like snow in the desert. Everything you had ever worked for fades. Everything just goes. Gone." He became silent.

"We have to help clean." Roberto broke the melancholy mood. "Is there anything you need before we go?"

Massimo smiled. "Yes, my life." He studied their confused faces. "Why are you here listening to an old man complaining about his life? You'll have plenty to complain about when you get older. For now, have some fun. Build memories. It's the only thing you'll have." The boys did not hesitate to leave.

As they ran past the kitchen on their way to join Uncle Sal at the garage they saw Mrs. Salutati and Maria in what looked like a serious conversation, but they only waved and kept going. Junk was far more of interest then what girls would talk about.

"Maria," Antoinette said just as Maria was taking two nougat candies.

"Yes?" Maria looked up.

"Please put the candies back."

Maria was confused. Who was she to tell her what to do? Only Mama and Uncle Sal could do that. Perhaps Yolanda if there was a good reason. "Why?"

"Because you have become a young woman." Her eyes continued to command her obedience.

"What does that mean?" Maria put back one of the candies.

"You are growing attractive to men and they will desire you as you desire that candy."

"Me? I'm too ugly and fat. Nobody would want me." She defied the older woman.

"Believe me when I tell you that those traits can be changed. I once was as you are." Antoinette remained with a stern expression.

"You?" Maria was incredulous. Before her stood an older, but very attractive woman with great hair, great figure, great clothes, and a beautiful face.

"Yes, me, but I had to learn how to eat properly, speak correctly, and to wear jewelry, cosmetics and clothes to my advantage. It's fun to learn and has great rewards. You said you were ugly. Well, you didn't finish the sentence. You are an ugly duckling. I'm sure you've heard the story."

Maria nodded still clutching her one nougat. "And by learning all those things I'll be a beautiful swan, right?"

"Exactly. With beauty and a smile, people, especially men overlook a lot of other faults." They stared at each other a moment. "Do you have a place where we won't be disturbed so that I can work my magic?" Antoinette lifted her purse. "Everything I need is in this little bag. All I need is fifteen minutes."

Maria hesitated not sure what Mama would say, but she thought that fifteen minutes wasn't a long time. "We can use my room upstairs...no...let's use the bathroom right here."

They went together. Maria's hair was gently brushed back with some staying spray, she was given a touch of lipstick, some rouge, some lines emphasized, and a subtle perfume was applied. Antoinette opened Maria's collar and placed a cheap pearl necklace around her neck. In less than fifteen minutes, Maria was transformed. The young girl looked carefully at herself in the mirror and liked what she saw except for one blatant feature. She was fat. She turned from the mirror to look at Antoinette. "I'm fat."

"I've done my magic, now it's time for you to do your magic."

Maria once again looked at herself in the mirror growing angry at what she saw. Angry, but determined. She began to tear up, but shook off the emotion. She stood. "Thank you, Mrs. Salutati. I see what I must do."

"But wait, Maria. You haven't heard the best news. As you start your magic, my magic gets even better." She smiled for the first time.

Maria smiled back as she walked to the kitchen to throw the candy back in the dish. "It's time for me to become a swan."

"Yes, indeed it is."

Chapter 23

Marcello and Yolanda reached the bocce court at the back of the grocery just as the reddish crescent moon had cleared the line of trees. To the left of them was Felizia, the bakery and to the right was Minnicks, a general store that specialized in bait and tackle. The stores were closed but each had a light in front except for the Bacci's which had one in the back to show the playing area. Marcello talked about the game, his parents, their connections to important people, and the trade business.

Yolanda stifled a yawn. "You seem very interested in the business."

"Sure, why not? You take care of business and business will take care of you. I like having money to buy the things I like, but I'm a fair person, you'll see." They slowly walked around the court, Marcello getting closer to Yolanda.

"This would make an interesting picture. A crescent moon with a bright star over the bocce court. Stars have always fascinated me because they seem so eternal. I was told once that even in the day the stars are there. I could paint a mural of this scene on the wall if your dad would let me." Yolanda could sense that there was something special in the air. It was soft and comforting.

Marcello leaned toward her and kissed her on the cheek. He wanted more but Yolanda was nervous. She wasn't sure if she wanted to be involved. It could be risky. Everything was there for romance but something held her back. Marcello turned her to face him and she stared into his eyes. They were going to kiss.

"Marcello." A figure they had not seen was standing at the far end of the court. "I'd like to practice."

"Dante, what are you doing here?" Marcello stepped back from Yolanda.

"Practicing by starlight. Are you still working on that toilet?" Dante asked waiting for them to clear the court.

"Oh, Yolanda, this is my older brother, Dante. He goes to college. He's named after the poet that went to hell. Dante wants to be a teacher. Not much money in that." Yolanda nodded a recognition.

"Yolanda, is it?" asked Dante slowly. "Well, Yolanda I like your idea of the mural, but my dad won't like it. It's too arty for him."

"Oh?" Yolanda was getting irritated. "Your brother thinks it's a good idea."

"And so do I." Dante threw one of the balls and got within four inches of the pallino. "I said my dad won't like it. Anything but a photo is too arty for him."

"How do you know that?" Yolanda asked purposely standing closer to Marcello.

"Because I've already asked to do one in the style of Giotto and was turned down."

Yolanda stared at him then at Marcello. "So you're named after a poet that went to hell?"

"There's more to it than that. It involves his love for a beautiful girl named Beatrice and Signor Dante also went to heaven."

"Did they get together after all that?" Yolanda asked glancing at Marcello.

"What do you think, Yolanda? If a man was willing to go to hell and back for you, could you turn him down, eh?"

"If he could have heaven, why would he want me?" She turned to Marcello. "I think it is time to go."

A second ball rolled up to Yolanda's foot which blocked an otherwise good shot. "Interference," Dante said. "I would have scored."

Marcello spoke. "But, Dante, she didn't mean to block your ball."

Dante moved from the shadows. "Of course interference is part of the game, isn't it? You get your ball close then try to block your opponent. That way it forces him to take a risk to score." He smiled a warmth that disturbed Yolanda.

"I don't like risk," she said.

"Perhaps you haven't wanted something strong enough for which you would take a risk." His dark eyes penetrated her decorum.

"Well...I..." She stopped to gather her thoughts. "So you want to be a teacher? What kind?" Any topic than the one they were discussing.

"I hope to be a good teacher. My major is art." He carried a ball in his hand. "Ever bocce?" He moved close to Yolanda and handed her a ball. "It's easy. Try."

She took the ball from him staring into his eyes. His words could be taken in many ways. Was he trying to offend? "The pallino is right under me."

"Then all you have to do is drop something and win." Dante spoke to her but looked at his brother.

130

Yolanda dropped the ball on Dante's foot. "It seems I missed. Come on Marcello, it's time to leave."

They had taken a few steps when she turned back to see Dante watching them. "Better luck next time, Beatrice. With a little practice, I bet you'd be great at bocce."

Chapter 24

The day of the garage sale was a day seldom experienced in Baltimore in July because the humidity was low and the temperature moderate. Antoinette's advertising, Yolanda's decorations, the energy of Antonio and Roberto, and the constant supervision of Mama brought in a crowd of people willing to buy. Sal sold all of his excess vegetables, fruit, honey and eggs with the crowd pleasing word organic handwritten on every item. On one table hosted by Josephine, Maria and Dominic, there were pizzelles, pesto, pizza, and pasta along with a large pitcher of Sicilian lemonade which became so popular that a separate table was set up with Maria in charge. With Antoinette walking among the customers to be sure they were happy and Rosalina keeping an eye on order, cleanliness and theft, the sale was doing very well. What Rosalina noticed was that Maria refrained from samples and that several young men who could not have been that thirsty visited the lemonade stand on many occasions.

Massimo with a few phone calls and his business savvy managed to buy forty pounds of nuts and candies at promotional prices then repackaged them for sale at a five hundred percent mark up. When asked why he was growing a mustache he said that mustaches always grew. He said he was just not cutting it because he needed something to confuse the devil.

Everyone seemed to have their own space open to various specialties. At one stand decorated in yellow and red, the traditional colors of Sicily, Yolanda sold her paintings and offered to do portraits of people, pets, or places. Antonio had a place where people could sign up for lawn service or any odd job that needed basically slave labor. Roberto, having found an old but at one time very expensive camera, advertised to take photos of people dressed in old -fashioned clothes, which he had also found in a massive piece of luggage. Rifling through the suits, Roberto discovered that the wardrobe most likely had belonged to the Ulliono family of Cagliari, Sardinia. The passport was dated 1927. When Roberto asked Mama who it was, she told him that she had no idea. What disturbed her was the Fascist party membership card in the vest pocket.

Even Rudolpho showed up to sell crabs, giving part of the profit to Rosalina, and the Strassmyers complained of the noise, traffic and lack of permit, but nobody paid attention to them.

When Marcello arrived with his mother saying his father was too busy to take time for such things as garage sales, he introduced her to Yolanda and Rosalina. Mrs. Bacci smiled, bowed her head and made an excuse to walk about. She did not shake hands or take much recognition of Yolanda or her paintings. She was adorned in a long dark dress that had a subdued print of swirls, she wore very expensive jewelry, her hair had a perfect set, and she moved not as a successful man's wife, but as royalty. Everywhere she went, tended by Marcello, people moved aside and she bought nothing. Rosalina watched the woman carefully, and when she got Yolanda's attention she raised her eyebrows, but said nothing. Nothing needed to be said.

"I'll take that one," Dante said as he approached Yolanda's table pointing to the painting on the side of the garage. "Please have it wrapped."

"It's not for sale," Yolanda said continuing to watch Marcello and his mother strut about the yard. "Your mother is here," she said pointing to the couple.

"And so are you," Dante replied ignoring her gesture. He looked at her paintings. "These are very good. I know people with degrees in art that can't do as well, but you need to develop a sense of perspective."

"Things are for sale as they are." Yolanda finally turned to look at Dante wondering if he was talking in innuendos. Dante was stockier, hairier and darker than Marcello. Dante had a mystery about him that was fascinating and more wary than Marcello. He picked up a painting of a creek at sunset and pretended to listen to it. "What are you doing?"

"I can almost hear the fluttering of wings on the distant shore. I'll take this one. Perhaps one day you'll tell me why you chose to paint it. I particularly like your idea of the stars."

"I just painted it. It was a scene I liked." She shrugged.

"But Marcello isn't in it." Dante turned the picture around and looked at the back "No, not even here."

"Marcello isn't in any of my paintings. Why should he be?"

"My point exactly." He looked about him. "Hold this one for me, I want to take some pictures so don't go away." He smiled and Yolanda smiled back. How could she not?

Rolando came up to his mother just as she brought out a pot of Italian sausage. "Look, Mama, it's Gabe." He pointed to a boy in a green shirt next to two older people most likely his parents. He did indeed look a lot like Rolando.

Rosalina put the pot down in front of Dominic. "Dominic, these smell delicious. Did you put the card in front of the food so that everyone can see who made it?" Dominic pointed to a placard offering not only customized dinners, but European catering. She turned to Rolando. "So who's with him?"

"That's his parents. They hardly speak English."

Rosalina went over to them. "Scusi," she said," but I believe my son Rolando knows your son, Gabe. I'm Mrs. Raphaeli."

The man's eyes widened in surprise. "So, you Raphaeli. That Rolando. We be Crepiscus. Bruno come. Bad thing. We from Romania. I am Vladsic. Here my wife Portia." They shook hands.

"Gabe has impressed both Rolando and his sister, Francesca." She wanted to say more but Rosalina could see the language was already too difficult.

"You Italiana?" Portia asked holding her stomach.

"Si. I hear you go to doctor soon." Rosalina realized she was changing the way she talked that could be seen as condescending.

Portia nodded. "Everything okay? Sorry about dog."

Rosalina only nodded and smiled. "Is there anything you would like?" She motioned to the tables in a gesture of generosity.

Portia nodded. "Little glass to put food for winter."

Rosalina thought a moment. "Ah, yes, of course." She went to a table piled with miscellaneous boxes and pulled out one containing twenty-four mason jars and handed it to her.

"Yes. This is it. You do too?" Portia received the box and nodded to her husband to pay but Rosalina only held up her hand.

"It's a gift and yes, we use them too."

Portia nodded a 'thank you' as Gabe started to leave with Rolando. Vladsic blurted out, "No, Gabe, stay." He then spoke rapidly in Romanian to his son.

"They need me to translate," said Gabe. "I'm sorry Rolando but I must be here."

"Then I'll stay with you if that's alright with your parents," said Rolando looking up at the stern figure of Vladsic.

Gabe said something to his dad who nodded, smiled at Rolando, and then turned to Rosalina. "Very good boy. You have church?"

"Yes. It is Pentecostal." Rosalina was taken back at the interest knowing that Romanians are Orthodox.

"We come?" Vladsic only glanced at his wife knowing it was his decision. She nodded her approval

"You are very welcome. Don't bring Bruno." Rosalina stifled a smile.

"Bruno a demon. He needs church." His face was serious but slowly came a grin then a smile.

It was then that Sal noticed that his sister was talking to people that could only be the owners of Bruno. He wanted to meet them.

Chapter 25

"Salvatore Pasquali?" The question was asked in a rough gravely voice from one of the two well dressed men who approached Sal. It was the sort of question that came from someone who already knew the answer.

Sal did a quick evaluation. Nicely dressed, good haircuts, trim, and determined. He was going to give a cocky answer but changed his mind. "Yes, and you are...?"

"Interested in talking to you about something that requires privacy. Is there a place we can go?" the heavier one asked.

Sal wanted to scream all kinds of objections but only said, "Sure. Follow me. May I know what it is?"

"Avanti, signor. All will be explained," continued the thinner one.

Sal went up the stairs slowly to draw attention to himself. The two men followed him. At the top he opened the door and stepped aside allowing them to enter first giving him time to notice if anyone had taken notice of him. Marcello had. Sal pointed to Rosalina then made a quick motion of his thumb indicating he wanted her to come. When he joined the two inside he brought them to the chandelier room where it would be cool, quiet and private. He motioned for them to be seated on the green brocade Empire style chairs that matched nothing in the house.

"I'm sure you have names just as surely as you won't tell me who you are. All I ask is for you to remember I'm a family man who is having a garage sale to help out that family. Now, what can I do for you?"

"We're also family people, Signor Pasquali. We represent the syndicate, a firm from whom a guest in your house has borrowed a large sum of money that we would like returned. Are you familiar with this topic?"

"Shouldn't you be talking to Mr. Salutati? Sal remained standing offering nothing to drink.

"We have and he refuses to pay. We are not asking for you to pay, we are only asking that you talk to him."

"Look, I've talked to my sister about the situation and it seems he doesn't have the money. He needs time to..."

"He has assets. We only want what is ours." The heavy one spoke slowly staring at the chandelier with increased interest. "He has a bank."

"He won't sell. He's worked all his life for that bank. What could I possibly say to him to convince..."

The thin one interrupted, "We are trying to avoid unpleasantries for him, his wife, or anyone who would protect him." He removed his dark glasses to stare at Sal.

"Meaning me," Sal said.

"Meaning anyone," repeated the heavy one still evaluating the light fixture. "Look, he can keep his personal stuff; just sign over the bank. We've been very understanding." He stood and examined the arms of the chandelier.

The thin one glanced at his partner but spoke to Sal. "We know it's hard to lose something you worked for, but to lose your health over it? He thought he could run, but we ran faster. Try to convince him; it's his last chance." He reached into his suit pocket which Sal did not like and withdrew some folded papers and a pen. "All he needs to do is sign this and leave it on the bureau in his bedroom. We'll do the rest."

"In his bedroom?"

"Where we've been already," said the heavy one. He turned away from the light to face Sal. "Tell me, Mr. Pasquali, where did you get this lamp?"

Sal looked at the chandelier then at both of the men surprised at the change of topic. "It was my father's. He gave it to me when we came to America, why? Is there something special about it?"

"Who gave it to your father?"

"If you must know, a church in Cefalu, Sicily." Sal was getting confused. "Does this lamp have anything to do with Mr.Salutati?"

"Be patient, Mr. Pasquali. I'm coming to that." The heavy one looked at his partner who was also bewildered at the conversation. "Do you happen to know where this church got it? It doesn't look like a church object. Far too fancy."

Sal scratched his neck. "Now we are going back into history." He paced the floor glancing up at the two. One of the men waited. The other, only looked back and forth between his partner and Salvatore. "Ah, yes. The church was St. Leo's and from what I understood, the church received it from some count, I believe a Count Caldonuevo." Sal shrugged.

The thin one was about to say something when the heavier man held up his hand for him to remain silent. "Now why would a count do such a thing?"

"I don't know. All I know is that the church gave it to my grandfather for some work he did for the church." Sal shook his head. "Why all this about some lamp?"

"Yeah," the thin one spoke up, "why all this about a light, eh?"

"I want to give you a little history lesson. First of all it wasn't a count it was a baron and this baron wouldn't give anything to a church. This chandelier was stolen by some bandits from the hills—the Black Hand. I'm sure you've heard of them. That baron was in my family and the chandelier has been missing for years. And now here it is in front of me."

Sal looked at the piece with a new curiosity. The lamp had been something nobody wanted. That is how it ended up belonging to him and now the Black Hand? "How do you know that? What are the chances of your story having any facts that could be...?"

The man waved for Sal to get closer. "Do you see the hooks holding the crystals?" He pointed to them. "They are of silver and if you look even closer you will see five marks on those hooks even though it would be difficult now because they are not cleaned."

"If you can't see them, how do you...?" Sal removed one of the crystals with its holder and stared at the curved metal, rubbing it. As some of the dirt was worn off he saw some lines and what looked like a very small shield. "A shield?"

"Yes, a shield. It is our family coat of arms." The man withdrew his wallet and pulled out a card with the same design on it. "See, Signor Pasquali, the family arms of the San Giorgio."

Sal rubbed more to expose the five lines. "Now what? So you have a coat of arms. An object like this could have been legally bought on the open market." Sal suddenly felt defensive of the chandelier.

"I'd like to purchase this from you."

"It's...not for ...sale." Sal had no idea of why he had said that.

"We could just take it." The thin man rose to his feet. "Believe me when I say we have many ways of..."

"But it is for exchange," Sal added.

The two men looked at each other. "Exchange?" The heavier one started to smile. "A chandelier for a five million dollar write-off? Guess again."

"No, not for that. Let's say I convince Mr. Salutati to sell and you get this chandelier. I'd like a promise from you that you will use your powers of persuasion to set up Salutati's son, Dominic, in his own fully equipped restaurant. Agree?" Sal was confused as to what he was saying.

"And just what do you get?" asked the thin one. "We get the bank and this lamp, Dominic gets a restaurant, Salutati gets a chance to enjoy retirement and you lose the chandelier. What gives? Eh?"

"I get my room back and the gratitude of the syndicate for helping them to get what they wanted." What the hell am I talking about Sal wondered.

"I'm not sure I understand," said the heavy one. "Just convince him and I want the chandelier. Okay?"

"Sure. Now I have to get back to the sale. Why don't you try some of the pizzelles? They go well with the lemonade." Sal motioned for them to leave. "Let me put this crystal back. I'll be right there."

The two men walked slowly to the door and at the door the heavier man turned back. "Just be sure to talk to him. Make it easy for everyone and be careful with my chandelier, capise?"

When Sal turned to put the crystal back he saw another person looking at it. "Who are you? The sale's outside."

"My name is Dante Bacci, Marcello's brother and from what I heard there's plenty of trading going on inside as well." He smiled and extended his hand which Sal shook.

"You didn't answer my question." Sal was cautious.

"I was here to observe. To make sure you were okay."

"Okay? What are you talking about?"

"Marcello saw your signal and told your sister who in turn told Marcello to come here." Dante looked closely at the five marks nodding his head and speaking softly to himself, "It's amazing the coincidence, but it does happen. The point now is how to use the opportunity."

"So where is Marcello?"

"He's not the type."

"And you are the type. What sort of type would that be?"

Dante evaluated Sal. "I'm more dangerous than I look."

"Oh? And if they had tried..."

With a speed almost too fast to follow Dante withdrew a stiletto. "I'm very accurate."

"There ...were two...of them." Sal swallowed a bit shocked at Dante's action.

"I had the element of surprise. The question now is are you going to convince this Salutati? Much depends on your success."

Sal stepped back. "And what's that to you?"

"I'm more involved than you realize. Let me help."

Sal glanced at the shiny knife held in Dante's hand. "I'm not too sure I want..."

"I can be very gentle. Salutati just needs to see the larger picture. He has to see that by his son getting his own place, he can live with him and the operative word is live. It's no longer a question of money, but one of time. Time is not money, time is life." Dante rolled the stiletto and quickly placed it in his pocket with a smile.

"What do you get?"

"Your good wishes for any future endeavor I might plan where you can help." Sal was about to ask but Dante cut him off. "Don't ask, but know that what I plan is for the good of all."

"How can you be so sure you can convince Mr. Salutati to give up his bank?" Sal put the crystal back.

"I convinced you. Now let's leave. There are some people who want to see you walk out of here alive. Avanti."

Sal only shook his head and walked toward the back door. He turned to say something to Dante, but the room was empty.

As he went down the stairs Rosalina came up to him. "Sal?"

"Not now, Rosalina. Keep doing what you were doing. Everything is fine and I'll explain things later. Right now take care of the customers." As he spoke Sal kept looking around for the two syndicate men. He didn't see them but he did see that Antonio and Roberto had set up a small dining area for people to relax and a sold sign on the large mirror. Marcello said that the two men had paid top dollar for it and that they would be back later with a truck. Sal did not like the sound of that.

Chapter 26

When the sale was over, the garage nearly empty, the food consumed, and everyone exhausted, Rosalina said they had cleared over three thousand dollars with no taxes. Even the food tables were sold. Several people wanted to know about the shot gun blast of the camel and were told various stories, none of which were true but all of which were entertaining. It was then in the quiet of the evening that Sal decided to tell Rosalina about the two men.

Sal had taken a sip of his espresso when from upstairs they heard, "Help. Somebody, help. Massimo has fallen down. I think he's had a heart attack." It was Antoinette.

Rolando and Francesca were playing chess at the end of the table and Sam was practicing sounds in every language. Sal slowly stood feeling the strain of a long day. "Antoinette, what's happening?"

"He's on the floor and he's not moving." Her voice got louder as she yelled down the stairs.

"Is he breathing?" Sal and Rosalina went to the landing as the kids gathered to see what was happening. Roberto held a camera in his hand and Enzo, the new puppy was by Antonio's side.

Sal found Massimo breathing heavily and still but alive. "Rosalina," Sal said, "call the ambulance."

When Rosalina left, Antoinette handed Sal a note. "It was pinned to his pillow."

The note read: Nice family, nice children, nice day, and nice wife. Now be nice and sign. P.S. we got the mirror. All we need is the chandelier.

At the hospital they brought Massimo to a room equipped with every conceivable electronic gadget they could fit into a ten by eleven space and still have a patient. Tubes were attached, air supplied, and the machines hummed. When Sal was finally allowed to come in, the doctor with a name Sal could not pronounce said, "That was close. He'll be fine but he will need rest. Did something shock him?"

"It's a long story. May I talk to him?" Sal looked past the doctor at a sleeping Massimo.

"Not now. Are you related to him?"

"Not yet. Again it's a long story. Is there anything I can do?"

"For now, go home. Maybe tomorrow. If his wife wants to stay there is a chair that can be converted to a bed. It might be good that when he wakes he sees a friendly face." The doctor hesitated. "It will be a friendly face? He was saying something in another language. It might have been Spanish or Italian."

"Italian. He's visiting us from Italy." Sal really did not want to go into the topic.

"What part? The Italian was different from what I had heard when I was in Milano."

"Sicily."

"Sicily? He's not in trouble with the mafia, is he?" He smiled.

Sal only shrugged. "You watch too many movies."

It was several days before Massimo could be visited by anyone other than his wife and Sal. What surprised everyone was that Dominic did not visit his father. Sal thought here was a man willing to sacrifice everything for a son who did not even come to see him. Fate and flukes of life.

One evening at eight-twenty, twenty minutes after visiting hours, as Massimo prepared to watch television, he noticed a figure dressed in a doctor's uniform near one of the machines. "Oh, I did not see you, dottore. Is there something wrong? So far everyone has been very nice to me."

"My name is Dante Bacci. I'm a specialist and I need to talk to you about some post operation options." The figure came closer. He did not smell medicinal, but more like very expensive perfume. "I am here to persuade you to do something that would benefit your wife, your son, the Raphaelis, and of course you."

Massimo stared at him. "You are not a doctor."

The figure leaned over Massimo. "First of all, let me explain to you why I am not here. I am not here to harm you. I am here because I am in love with Yolanda, Rosalina's daughter. Keep that in mind no matter what I say."

"Yolanda? Yes, I know of her, but what does that..."

"Just listen and rest. Recently you were visited by the syndicate and given a note. They could have done a lot of damage, but they didn't and the reason was that those men had a talk with Sal and Sal had a talk with me. You've been the topic of a lot of conversations, Massimo. You're a very popular guy. Now listen very carefully. A proposition was arranged that said if you signed over the already defaulted bank with no other problems, the syndicate would arrange for your son, Dominic, to have his own restaurant. When this happens, Dominic will most likely ask Rosalina to marry him. You and your wife are off the hook, you get a daughter-in-law, the kids get a daddy, and you will have a place to live comfortably surrounded by your new grandchildren. Because you caused no trouble, the syndicate will allow you to go back to Sicily to get what money you can and get away from the place that stabbed you in the back. If you refuse, I will be forced to withdraw my protection."

"But my bank? My work?" Massimo turned toward Dante.

"Relax. If that monitor goes crazy you will miss the opportunity to do a great deal of good." Dante stepped back. "What about your bank? Your assets are gone, your son never wanted it and your wife feels threatened. Your bank is a problem."

Massimo rested on his pillow. "I was hoping I'd be remembered."

"By whom? Those creeps in Sicily? Massimo, they are nothing but greedy bastards and you know that. If you want to be remembered, then be remembered by a loving family who you helped. Help your son get his dream. Help the Raphaeli's children. Your future, Massimo is in the kids, not a bank. Do you even know their names? You should because they will remember your name long after the assholes have forgotten you."

Massimo was silent looking at some ad on T.V. "All my work..."

"Is for what you are about to do, not for what you've done. Sign the paper, then show them your ass after you get the money. Otherwise, you'd better like this little cramped room because you'll be here a lot."

"But what about the bastards in Sicily? The syndicate can't protect me all the time, eh? I need three days. I need three days of safety. Can you get me those days? Eh?"

"You won't see me, Massimo. At that I am excellent. If you need three days, you have three days. Right now I ..."

Massimo sat up. "Sal gets nothing. He loses his precious lamp. For what?"

Dante came very close to Massimo looking so deeply into the older man's eyes that he was taken back at the intensity. "Sal is a very rare person, Massimo. You see he loves and that love is his reward." Dante pulled out the folded contract. "Sign. You'll feel much better and you'll get a good night's sleep." He handed the man the paper with a Mount Blanc pen. Massimo looked at the sheets, then at the machines, the room, Dante and with a smile signed.

"Look," said Dante, "your blood pressure has already gone down." He took the contract from Massimo and moved quietly to the door where he was met by an incoming nurse.

"Oh, doctor, I didn't know you were in here. I noticed a change in the pressure so I..."

"He's doing very well. He is a man who is loved by many so take good care of him." He turned to the reclining figure. "Bonne notte, mei amico. Sto bene. Arreviderci."

Massimo looked up at the ceiling with a contented look on his face. "Grazie. Tante grazie por mei vito." Thank you for my life.

Chapter 27

The brick shithouse fell in on the twentieth of July, just two days before the bocce tournament. It was a surprise to Sal, who had never had that happen before, but it was a shock to the two inside. When Sal asked Marcello about how he had prepared the mud he discovered Marcello had reversed the amount of sand and cement. Though the owner, Mr. Bacci screamed profanities, Sal assured him that everything would be set right before the games even if it meant working round the clock. He was reminded by Mr. Bacci that he would receive no extra money even though it was his son who made the mistake. Through it all, Sal took the news in stride. He was not going to have his reputation ruined because someone reversed numbers.

Antonio, seeing his uncle do extra work so that he could take a gun course, dropped the course to help his uncle. Marcello was not allowed to help because his mother said he was needed elsewhere to prepare for the bocce contest. Very rapidly Antonio learned to mix and carry allowing his uncle to just build. Dante as well as Mr. Salutati had simply disappeared. All that Antoinette would say was that her husband had been very quiet for a few days muttering things like 'I can do this' and 'It's for the best' and most ominous of all 'I just hope I come back in one piece.' The Bacci's never understood Dante so his vanishing was one more mystery.

As uncle and nephew worked and sweated together Sal asked where Enzo was. "Did you get rid of him when you dropped the course?"

"Of course not. He's with Tino. They get along great together." Antonio had been watching his uncle very carefully. "I was wondering if I could do some building."

"Sure. You just have to be careful of a few measurements to keep it level, and then it's up you go. Let me show you." The two worked into the evening and Mr. Bacci was so impressed, rather shocked, at the progress that he offered both of them some lemonade. It did not compare to Dominic's.

Yolanda showed up in late afternoon to find out if they would be home for dinner and was told, not tonight. "Where is Marcello? He should be out here with you. He made the mistake."

Antonio spoke. "He's inside with his mother making cookies or some such things: that's why I'm here to make sure the job is done right." He looked at his uncle with a smirk.

"That's right, Antonio," Sal said wiping his brow with a small towel.

"Inside?" Yolanda stared at the closed door. "Where it is air conditioned and you outside in the heat when it was him who made the..." She stopped and stormed into the store leaving the door open.

Antonio and Sal heard yelling. First Yolanda then Mrs. Bacci then Yolanda like a see saw. "Antonio, keep working. You can listen but this job must get done."

Then came the deep voice of Mr. Bacci, then Mrs. Bacci screaming. Yolanda burst out raising her hands into the air. "Stupido. They are all stupid." Immediately following Yolanda Mrs. Bacci came out, yelling about how Yolanda had schemed to take away her son. The woman stood there screaming after Yolanda when Antonio lifted a large glob of mud and put it on her left shoe.

She stopped screaming and looked at the mud. "What have you done? These are very expensive hand crafted leather shoes from Milano."

"It was a mistake. You walked directly into where I was working." Antonio was not convincing.

"Mistake? Mistakes. All you Raphaelis ever have is mistakes. Look what you did to a simple job of a toilet. Ah, you can't even build that." She glared at Antonio.

At that Antonio threw down the trowel. "My uncle is the best brick layer. How dare you criticize him when..."

"Antonio." Sal spoke in a firm deep but soft voice. "Antonio? Antonio?"

The young boy, still excited turned abruptly "What?" He then realized he was talking to his uncle. "Excuse me, Uncle Sal. What is it?"

"It doesn't matter what you or anyone else says about my work. The proof is in the result. Now work. Your hands will show what your mouth can not." He looked at Mrs. Bacci "The building will be done this evening. I hope it meets your satisfaction and we are deeply sorry about your shoes."

Mrs. Bacci looked at both of them, the building then her shoes. "Well, it better be good." She limped off to the house leaving a small trail of wet like a slug.

The day of the tournament was sweltering. More than the prize of a free trip to Italy brought out the competitors. It was for the green ribbon of victory and the bragging rights. At the last moment Marcello was asked to stand in for an absent Dante, but Marcello knew he was no substitute. When Dante finally arrived looking very worn he was told by his mother that Marcello had taken his place. Dante only shrugged and walked away. That's when he saw Yolanda.

"I thought you were on the team," Yolanda said. Where have you been?"

"I thought I was on the team, too, but Marcello is taking my place." He came close to Yolanda. "I had to go to Italy for a few days to help Mr. Salutati."

Yolanda stared in disbelief. "You went to Italy?" She thought a moment noticing how tired Dante looked. "Why aren't you on the team? Marcello is not as good as you."

Dante only smiled at the comment. "My mother wants to see Marcello and to be honest, I don't really care. It's just a game and they're always changing the rules. Does Marcello look fifty? Did you notice the new jerseys? I got them for our team. Sometimes you play a better game when you dress up a bit. Don't you agree?"

"I never know how to take what you say, Dante." She kept looking at him wondering how she felt. There was something different about him. There was something of the mystic in the way he talked. "Do you really like my paintings even if they lack perspective?"

"Every day a little more." They stood watching the teams play on the three courts.

"You've studied art at college, right?" Yolanda asked still watching the games.

"Yes, a great deal of art, why?"

"You have models. I mean like real human models?" She turned to face Dante.

"Of course. How else can you understand the anatomy?"

"Are there male models?"

"All kinds, sizes, shapes, colors, and religions."

"And they are nude?"

"As a jay bird." Dante knew the idea was alien to her. And everyone can see...well..." Yolanda turned away.

"All the angles, curves, textures, lines, and shadows of the naked human body. It's a symphony of silent sounds. The naked body is not sexy, Yolanda. Doctors can tell you that. What's sexy is the soft touch of a finger on the cheek," which he did to Yolanda, "and the look of passion in the eyes." Dante looked deeply into Yolanda's eyes so that he could see his own reflection and she hers.

Yolanda held her breath then turned as she exhaled. "Uncle Sal said you were helpful with Mr. Salutati when he was in the hospital."

"Your Uncle Sal was in the hospital?"

"What? Oh, you and your...well...ways. No, what I..."

"I tried. He just needed a friend. He's fine now and so will a lot of people be." Dante pointed to the court. "Ah, it's Marcello's turn. I wish him the best for Mom's sake." Dante was looking at Marcello, but Yolanda was looking at Dante. Marcello's ball missed by two feet. "Marcello missed."

"I know." She moved closer to Dante. "I want to be a good painter. Will you teach me perspective?"

"I think the lesson has already begun." He pulled her close to him and they kissed.

As they kissed, a mother with two girls passed near and one of the girls, about eight, turned to watch. For that she got a bop on the head. "Later. You'll learn that later."

Dante pulled her very close and they kissed again but longer.

Marcello got a new bocce ball realizing he was not doing well. He heard his mother encouraging him. He saw Dante and Yolanda kiss. He then threw the ball with such velocity that in ended in another court, hitting several balls disrupting that game. People laughed, cussed and taunted as he left the court. His mother came toward him, "Marcello why did you...?"

"Oh, just shut up," he said as he went inside.

Chapter 28

Rosalina stood there staring at the empty garage. The grapes were beginning to ripen, the berries were being picked each day, the eggs were at their best and the land was fertile. In a fenced in area were Sam and his favorite toys as well as Francesca. At the rear of the property she could see Sal working the garden. 'He is a good man. He's waiting for me to marry before he even looks for a new wife. He loves the children. What is he building? It looks like a wall.' Rosalina stared at the garage.

Rolando walked by on his way to help Uncle Sal. "Rolando, go get a tape ruler. I want to know exactly how big the garage is." Beyond big, Rolando really didn't care about size but he went. Adults always had strange requests and who was he to question the people who fed him? So he went.

Sal noticed the attention his sister was giving to the garage as he walked up to her. "Rosalina, you've been staring at this garage for half an hour. What is it? I can't build my compost pile while I see you pacing up and down. What's wrong?"

"Sal, I'm a widow. I have eight children. When they took the chandelier, which by the way I never liked, I somehow lost touch with Italy." She faced him as Rolando came up with the ruler. "Are you ever going to get married?"

"Rosalina, we've been over this." He took the ruler from Rolando and waved for him to go away. Just as Rolando turned Sal called to him. "Why did you bring me this ruler?"

"It's for Mama. She wants to know the size of the garage."

"Oh, okay and thank you. You can dig the rocks out of that pile of dirt." He turned back to Rosalina. "Why do you want to know how big the garage is?"

"You didn't answer my question." Rosalina stared at her brother.

"Okay. I will marry when I know you and the children are taken care of. I made a promise to Mama and Papa that I would do that. What is really bothering you?"

"Sal, our church is too small for us in the city and the rent is too high. I want to build a church here." She folded her arms over her waist. It was a sign she was determined. At this point Sal knew that reasoning had become second to feelings. Now reasoning was the servant of the emotions and spiritual emotions were the strongest.

"Here? My God, Rosalina. What of the neighbors? They already think we're nuts. This will prove it. Your old church is in the city. How will they get here? Eh?"

"The bus goes very close to us. They can get off at Minnicks and walk."

"In the rain and snow?"

"Maybe we can arrange transportation, I don't know. All I know is that we have this spacious unused building and the church needs it. All I know is that my children are beginning to go their separate ways." She stood staring at the painting of Moses. "Antonio is busy crapping and has Enzo, Yolanda is getting interested in painting and has Marcello or is it Dante. I can't follow what is happening. Maria spends her day dressed up and soon the boys will come. The old ways are slipping from me, Sal. I need something solid, like a church to ...to... I don't know. I don't need your criticism. I need your help." She turned to face her brother who was nodding. She was about to speak when she noticed a large man wearing a tee shirt reading 'Long live dynamite' and jeans of a peculiar color coming around the corner of the house.

"So there you be. I've been knocking on your front door. Are you ...Salvatore Pascalli or something like that?

"Something like that," Sal responded moving cautiously toward him. What now?

"I got a delivery for you." He turned and walked back to his truck. Sal watched as the man raised the door at the back of the truck and went inside. Within a moment he heard an engine start and out rolled a good size John Deere tractor which the man drove up to Sal and Rosalina. He turned off the engine, handed Sal the keys and said, "Jest sign on the bottom line and she's all yours."

Sal continued to watch in silence as the truck drove away leaving him the tractor, three five gallon containers of gas, and a trailer attached to the tractor. He watched as the truck turned the corner to disappear.

"Did you order this?" Rosalina touched the steering wheel.

"This? This? Rosalina this would cost over fifty thousand dollars. No, I did not order this. I'm not even sure it's mine. I just signed for something for which I could go to jail. No, I did not order this."

Rolando wandered up. "That's a very nice tractor you have, Uncle Sal. Can we all get in the back and take a ride?"

"Sure, sure, why not? But first I have to find any paper saying it belongs to me or some idea who sent this to me." Sal spoke as if in a dream. He found nothing until Rolando pointed to a note attached to the mirror. Sal thought, 'mirrors, always mirrors.' It was from the Garibaldi Franchise of Palermo. It read: Grazie, signor. Next time in Italy visit us. Sal knew it was a front operation for the syndicate. He looked over the machine losing himself in the projects he could do.

It was then Sal realized his sister had been talking to him. "...and Yolanda can decorate the church. I'll play the piano, we can bake cookies and all pitch in."

"What piano, Rosalina?" Sal asked absent minded still in awe over this gift.

"We'll get one. The family needs to work together on one project." Rosalina spoke happy words but her face was sad, even dejected.

"What's wrong, Rosalina?" Sal brought his mind from the tractor to his sister.

"Things are changing and sometimes it's hard to face the change." She looked at her brother. Her eyes were filled with sorrow. "You know I never go back to the garden. I don't go past the garage. The reason is I don't want to see Theresa and be reminded of Giorgio. I miss Mama and Papa. I miss Giorgio. The chandelier is gone and all the junk that Giorgio had in the garage is gone. The past is past and soon Yolanda will leave, too." She held up her hand. "A mother can tell, Sal. I can see a change in her eyes. She doesn't know it yet, but it's there." She took a deep breath that swallows sorrow. "I know, I know. It's natural, but I feel I'm coming apart. I need something solid."

Sal put his arm around his sister looking at the garage. "That's where I saw it."

Rosalina looked up at her brother bewildered. "Saw what?"

"Paolo Dondi has it covered up in his shed. I could probably get it for putting a shower in his back yard for the kids." Sal nodded as he spoke.

Rosalina pulled away from her brother. "What are you talking about, Sal? What's in Paolo's shed?"

"The piano, Rosalina. Paolo Dondi has an old upright with a bunch of scrolls and he wanted me to put a shower in for the kids so that they could rinse off before coming inside."

Rosalina stared at her brother wondering how serious he was. "So you think it's possible to have a church here? I thought you thought that would be crazy. You know the neighbors and all that."

"Why not? I've never been to this kind of church. I might like it. They believe in God, right? They have priests? They have blessings and songs? It's a church, eh?" he looked around thinking of the Strassmyers who were so Christian they hated everyone. "Who knows, maybe some of the neighbors will come over for at least the cookies and the espresso."

"It's a Pentecostal church. We have lots of singing, and praying and lots of people who will not believe God has given them..." She looked at Sal as tears started to form in her eyes.

Sal held her in his arms thinking of all that needed to be done smiling that a gift from the syndicate could be a major tool in building a church. So much of life is fate. A little hard work and fate. "Let's see what the children think of building our cathedral, okay?" She only nodded.

The Salutatis stayed long enough to pack what they could, thank the Raphaelis for their hospitality, and leave to live at the rear of their son's new restaurant located in Heron Point, a very fashionable section of town. For what he could scrounge and get for his house, Mr. Salutati had enough to get started in an improvement corporation to loan money to the locals for various projects. Because of his inconceivably low overhead, the interest rates were competitive. For the first time since they had come to America the Salutatis seemed happy.

Chapter 29

Dante showed up for dinner listening carefully to what Rosalina was saying about starting her own church. He thought it strange but couldn't say why. All Dante knew was that he was in love with Yolanda and if her family needed help, he was there to give it.

Rosalina talked to the children. "It would have to look like a church. We would have music, some food for after the service, decorations, a place for the pastor to preach, and chairs. All of us will have to pitch in. Uncle Sal will need help in building things and we need to do a lot of painting."

"What about a bathroom?" asked Maria. It was something no one had asked.

"Well...I...suppose they'll have to come inside the house until we build one in the church," answered Rosalina not happy with the answer.

"Then everyone in the church can hear you go," continued Maria.

"There'll be too much noise to hear you," Mama retorted.

"But," Antonio added, "we could put in a microphone just for you so they wouldn't miss what you do."

"Antonio," Mama said, "can't you be serious?"

As they were talking, Sal was figuring on what else would be needed. Certainly a fence to keep people from the garden and Theresa's grave.

"I have paintings we could put up," Yolanda said, "and the entire place needs to have the nails taken out and repainted." She paused a moment 'We need something religious like a cross."

"A cross?" asked Roberto.

"Well..." Mama seemed hesitant. "Maybe a small one. I don't want to talk about Jesus' death. I want to talk about his ideas and his miracles and his hope for all the beaten down people. You know what I mean?"

"He liked children, didn't he?" asked Francesca.

"Oh, very much," Mama smiled. "You got the idea."

"And he healed people of their illness, right?" asked Josephine.

"That's right," encouraged Mama. "Even people who could not see." There was silence as each person tried to remember the stories they had heard.

"He didn't like the rich, did he?" asked Roberto.

"He liked everyone. What he didn't like was that the rich thought more of their money than they did other people." Mama was happy that everyone was adding something.

"And," Dante spoke up, "did he not bring the dead back to life. He conquered death." He shook his head. "Quite a man." Rosalina said nothing but thought about Dante's words and her little Theresa. Yolanda turned toward him, once again wondering who Dante really was.

Rolando broke the silence. "He liked animals."

Sal, who had been lost in his calculations, finally spoke. "Yes, Rolando, he did. He even chased the people out of the temple because they were going to sacrifice the birds."

"Wouldn't it have been great if they had taken pictures of everything Jesus did, then we could see for ourselves what had happened," Roberto said holding up his camera.

Dante turned to Roberto. "That is a great idea."

"But he's dead," Roberto said.

Before Dante could respond, Rosalina said, "No. He is alive right now." The look on Rosalina's face said it all.

"But..." objected Antonio, "he died on the cross with the nails and spear."

"They never found the body, Antonio," said Dante. "He went straight to heaven with his body."

"Now that is the tough part of religion," said Sal. "That is faith. Some people have it and some don't."

"Where did he go?" Josephine asked.

"He went to heaven to be with his father," said Rolando.

"That's what we are all going to do, right, Mama, when we die? We can see Daddy again," Francesca said as if it were a done deal.

Then Maria added, "We'll see Theresa too. That will be very nice."

Rosalina started to cry. "Si, mei bambina, si." They all looked at Mama each having the same longing but they remained quiet.

Sal began to think of his own children and wife. He thought of being with them again. They would be together in a warm sunny land and the children would come to him asking, "Where have you been, Papa? We missed you.'

No vote needed to be taken. Everyone knew that Rosalina's church would be built.

After dinner Dante and Yolanda went to the front porch. There was a swing and some plants had been placed on the steps to make sure they got plenty of sun. It was a warm night and the only light came from a street lamp about a hundred feet away so that the shadows were deep and if one took the time the milky way was visible. Dante sat on the banister giving Yolanda the swing. "So your Mama is going to have a church," Dante said. "I have an idea about what she can put on the walls. She doesn't like talking about death so instead of the Stations of the Cross, I want to do the stations of the miracles."

"Stations of miracles?" Yolanda was curious.

"I have several friends who can help but Roberto will be the main man because he has the camera. One of my friends looks so much like the idea of Jesus he's even called J.C. He will be our model. We will show him curing the blind, making bread and wine, walking on water, and being with children. We can get someone to play Peter and the rest of the disciples."

"Who will play Judas? No one will want that," Yolanda said thinking of herself as Mary and Maria as the adulteress.

"That's a job for me. I'll put on a hat and no one will notice."

"Are you going to advertise for parts?"

"Why not? It's a photograph, no memorizing of lines." They were both silent for a moment. Then Dante smiled and said, "I suppose I could be the tempter in the desert."

"You know a lot about the Bible, Dante," Yolanda said.

"Before I became an art major, I did have other plans."

"Like what?"

"Like I wouldn't be here tonight with you."

"A priest?" Yolanda sounded surprised.

"There are other choices but, yes, a priest."

"What happened?"

"Enrico Pissano. He was a priest. He said I took a far too active role in my prayers, and that my sense of justice was too impatient for surrendering to God."

"Was he right?"

"I'm more dangerous than I look," Dante said with a smile. "You know I was named after a man who supposedly managed to go through hell and come back with a good story."

"I'm not familiar with the story," said Yolanda. She wanted to change the topic. "Dante, why does your mother dislike me?"

Dante leaned forward placing his foot on the floor. "It's a long story but basically my Mom, who is from Rome, dislikes anyone who is not Italian or Catholic. It's not you, Yolanda."

"But I am Italian," Yolanda objected.

"Not in her eyes. You're Sicilian and a Sicilian is right there with the Jews, the Negroes and the liberals. Believe me, this church of your mother's will be the clincher."

"Such prejudices," Yolanda frowned.

"It's not just her. Why do you think the Salutati's were ganged up on and driven out of Sicily? They were northerners. You see the prejudices works both ways."

"Do you feel that way about me?" Yolanda asked

Dante slipped off the banister, gently raised Yolanda and kissed her, holding her close to his body so that she could feel the strength of his muscles, the passion in his kiss, the pressure of his body against hers. He slowly pulled away kissing her on the cheek and neck before staring at her closed eyes, which opened in a dreaming way.

"I think I understand what the priest meant. Well, I want more." And under a canopy of stars Dante obliged her.

Chapter 30

Work on the church began the next day. A large container of lemonade was made and Rosalina, despite the heat, though it was cooler in the basement made quantities of pizza. In the midst of cleaning out what little remained in the garage Roberto found a piece of canvas with a picture wrapped in plastic. He asked Dante, who was removing all the nails, what it was. Dante at first dismissed anything that would stop him from his job but when the nails were finally out he took the package from Roberto and slowly unwrapped it. He could smell the odor of candle and the years of a musty basement. This was old and the picture was faded and cracked. "This, my brother, is a piece of history. I can't tell you everything but I think it's important." He slowly wrapped it back up in the plastic. "A certain professor needs to see this." He took the object and placed it in one of the saddle bags of his scooter. Except for long trips, for which Dante preferred the train, his Vespa was silent, cheap, durable, and highly maneuverable. In one saddle bag was his lunch and tools, the other was for cargo.

Sal blocked off an area for the raised platform, framed it, then roughed it in. The fence to protect the garden proved easier. He had lots of chicken fencing and stakes. It would do until a sturdier barrier could be built. He then called Paolo Dondi. Paolo was a widower with two children. The first was a boy, eleven, named Joseph; the second a girl, eight, named Veronica. His wife had died three years ago of cancer and he was doing the best he could. People encouraged him to date but he told them he wasn't ready. Sal and Paolo made the deal over the phone with Paolo agreeing to bring the piano late in the afternoon. Sal said by then the shower would be in. Even as he worked on the church, Sal, as did Rosalina, kept an eye on the children. Antonio was cutting someone's lawn while Roberto continued clearing the garage, and Dante checked for structural damage. Francesca was with Sam. Sam? Where was he? Where were Francesca and Rolando? He saw Yolanda mixing two buckets of paint. "Yolanda?"

"Yes, Uncle Sal."

"Where are Rolando, Francesca and Sam? They were supposed to be in the play area."

Yolanda looked around. "I'll go look in the house." Dante came out of the garage, when he heard Yolanda say to him, "The children are missing. Don't tell Mama. Look for them." She continued running to the house.

"A moment, Yolanda," Dante said pointing to something in the grass. "What is that?"

"It's a toy, haven't you ever seen a toy?" She turned back to the house.

"But it's away from the play area toward the woods. Look another toy, near the doll house." Dante moved quickly like a panther across the lawn; Yolanda could not keep up. "Ah, there's another. They're heading to the woods." Yolanda strained her eyes to see what Dante saw.

"Uncle Sal," Yolanda yelled. He looked up. "There're going to the woods. We'll get them." He waved back.

They found the three next to the spring. Rolando was talking to Francesca as Samuel played in the water. Yolanda came up to the peaceful scene. "We were worried about you; why did you come here?"

"Its nice here," said Francesca. "It's quiet."

Rolando looked up at his older sister. "We didn't mean to worry you, it was hot and Samuel was fussy."

"Aren't you afraid of Bruno?" asked Yolanda.

"Who is Bruno?" asked Dante looking about.

"A mean big dog that should be in prison," said Yolanda.

"I... I ...never thought about that." Rolando looked in the direction of Bruno. "What would you do if Bruno came?" Rolando asked Dante.

"Point to where Bruno would be," said Dante.

"There by the tree with a crooked branch." Rolando said.

In a single rapid and smooth motion Dante brought out his stiletto and stuck it at the base of the tree.

"You would kill him?" asked Francesca.

Samuel watched Dante throw the knife and ran after it, but Dante in a few steps retrieved the knife long before Samuel could get to it. "No I wouldn't kill him, I would hit him in the foot to remind him to be nice. He would limp home." Yolanda was impressed with Dante's skills but it concerned her that he was that good with a knife.

As the kids were in the woods, Sal decided to pick up Paolo Dondi. The piano was rolled out of the truck and placed in a garage that had received a first coat of paint for the inside. Pizza and lemonade were brought out so that everyone could eat in the shade of the grape arbor. Paolo had brought his two kids and as the adults ate, the kids became acquainted. Paolo was an electrician and he liked the idea of a church. In fact he himself would go to church since his children needed something to do in the summer. As they chatted, ate, and drank, Rosalina looked at Veronica realizing that the little girl was the same age as Theresa.

"Isn't that true, Mama?" asked Josephine.

"What? I...wasn't paying attention Josephine. What did you say?"

"I said we're going to feed the people after the service, right?"

"Yes, of course. It gives everyone a good feeling." She turned to Paolo. "Does your little girl do well in school?"

"Very. I'm proud of her." He smiled. "I just wish she had a mother. But who would want a fifty-two year old man with two children?"

"They don't come knocking at the door, do they?" Rosalina said thinking of her own situation. "You have to look."

"I'm a simple man. I work hard, I pay my taxes, I vote, I take care of my kids and I believe in God. I don't have time to go out to the bars. Besides, I don't want to go anyway."

"Same here," said Rosalina. She turned to Sal. "Did you get the shower in?"

"Yes Rosalina," Sal said taking a sip of lemonade. "And after that I built the platform, put up the fence, did the gardening, and started to build Mr. Smithington's wall. Maybe I'll put the electric in the church."

"What do you do in your spare time?" asked Dante, who had just walked up.

Sal raised his right arm to his chin and flicked it in the direction of Dante. "Eh, Patso." It was a Sicilian gesture meaning that the other person was crazy.

"What wall are you talking about?" asked Rosalina.

"It's for Smithington. He saw the job I did for Bacci and he called me. How he knew my number I'll never know, but the money will pay for improvements to the church." Sal looked over to see Antonio acting like a cripple for the other kids' amusement. "Antonio, what are you doing?"

"I'm practicing being a cripple."

"Are you planning to have an accident?" asked Sal.

"I will be healed," Antonio said.

Sal looked at Paolo. "I can't figure them out, can you?" He turned back to Antonio. "Who will heal you?"

Dante who had enjoyed the repartee finally said, "It's for a set of pictures Roberto is taking. A friend of mine will play Jesus and we'll get other people to play different parts. Antonio has volunteered to be a cripple.

"What parts are available?" asked Paolo.

"Every part," Dante said "Pick a person from the gospels, dress up, get photographed, and the best shots will go up in the church to show the miracles." Roberto takes the photos and Mrs. Raphaeli will be the judge.

"I know who Peter should be," said Antonio. "Rudolpho. He's big and he's a fisherman just like Peter.

"Dante said he would play the devil," said Yolanda.

"I want to be Mary and I think Maria will be an excellent Mary Magdalene."

"Do you mean the one who committed adultery?" asked Maria.

"The very one," said Dante.

"Good." Maria smiled.

"I want to be the donkey Jesus rode," said Rolando.

"Will you be Martha?" asked Yolanda of Francesca.

"Was she nice?"

"Very."

"Then yes, I'll be Martha."

"I'll be Pontius Pilot," Sal said, "then I can wash my hands of the whole thing."

"Would you like to be in our story?" Antonio asked Paolo.

"I'll be John the Baptist." He said softly.

"But he lost his head." Rosalina said turning to face him.

"That, Rosalina, is a small price to pay for being a friend of the son of God," Paolo said glancing about him.

"That was a good answer, Mr. Dondi," said Roberto. Dante nodded his approval.

Rosalina looked closely at her guest. "Yes it was. I'm very happy you are helping us with the church."

"I'll do better than that. I'll put in the electricity for you."

"I can't pay for that," said Sal.

"Here's my deal," said Paolo. "Any day I work for you, you have to provide dinner for the kids and me. Deal?"

"Sure" said Sal continuing, "I look forward to it."

"Great," Maria yelled out. She liked Veronica.

Yolanda leaned against Dante "Did you have anything to do with Uncle Sal's new job with the...uh ..."

"Smithingtons?" Dante asked "He wanted his son in the photo shots and I think you're beginning to know me."

Rosalina leaned toward Paolo "So you believe in God?"

"At this point in my life, Rosalina, He is the only thing I believe in." He gently touched Rosalina on the wrist in a gesture of friendship then removed it.

"She looked down at the spot where Paolo had touched her, and thought 'No. No. This can't be happening to me. No. Not now.' But it was.

Chapter 31

Through the warm days of late July and August, through the heavy rains and one terrible wind storm the work preceded. Dominic had stopped by the house one rainy day, inviting all of them to a dinner at his new restaurant named Massimo's after his father.

When the family arrived at the resaurant, they saw that Massimo's had three floors and the entire upper room was devoted to the Raphaeli family. He had prepared everything himself, including his favorite, Spaghetti Caruso, a Neapolitan dish. He sat down and asked what they were doing.

"We're making a church," said Francesca.

"A church?" Dominic sat back in his chair. "Really? A church? Who do you pray to?" He smiled.

"We pray to God," Roberto said.

"Which God is that?" Dominic asked. He turned to Sal, "Are you in this too, Sal?"

"Of course, I'm in the family." Sal cleared his throat. "Where are your mother and father? Are they too busy to visit?"

"He's not feeling very well, and so Mom is staying with him." Dominic turned to Dante. "I heard you were a big help to my father in Sicily."

"I gave him some time to do what he needed to do." Dante did not want to say more.

"I heard you were very persuasive."

"I'm glad it turned out fine."

"As a matter of fact he did very well in his business transactions. He made enough money to start a business here. He owes you a lot."

"Glad I could help. I'm sure he'll return the favor one day if I ever need it, right?"

"Sure. Anytime."

Yolanda listened to this disjointed conversation knowing more was being said than the words. It was all so vague, and she didn't know why.

"Anyway," Dominic said, "What about this church? What kind is it?"

"Pentecostal," said Rosalina.

"Is that like the holy rollers? You know people who speak in tongues?" Dominic was beginning to sound sarcastic. "Personally, I never go to church. I find them to be fanatics. You have to take religion in small doses."

"Fanatic?" questioned Yolanda. "What do you mean?"

"There are some who have to go to church every week. Sometimes twice a week. All they do is talk about God. They want to surrender their lives to the church. They do whatever the church tells them to do. And for what? A promise of heaven? A fictitious place? You're better off putting your energy into the real. Trust in science or maybe art but religion is too...I don't know. It's not solid, not creative, not joyful." Dominic looked around at everyone looking at him. "Well that's one man's opinion."

"Then," Yolanda said, "Tell us about the person who goes to his place of worship five or six times a week, listens absolutely to the high priest, carries an image of his God everywhere he goes, and sacrifices everything to that God?" asked Yolanda.

"I certainly would, but I don't know anybody like that, do you?" Dominic asked.

"Millions. That's what the majority of people do everyday, and for what Dominic? A maybe future? They are relying on a system where their savings and investments could vanish overnight. Look at your dad."

Dominic was about to say something but took a deep breath. "Look, all of you came here to enjoy a meal. Then enjoy it. If you want to build the church, then build it. I have my church right here."

After the meal Dante drove Yolanda home on the Vespa and as they drove, Yolanda asked, "How did you help in Sicily?"

"I just explained to certain people that Salutati needed some cash to get out of Sicily. That's what they wanted and that's what he wanted so they even helped to get him out."

"You always talk in riddles, Dante. Let me be blunt. Did you use that knife of yours to convince people?"

"Not directly, Yolanda, a little demonstration is all most people need." He was quiet for a little while, then added "They were bad people doing bad things and they knew it. I helped balance the injustice."

"Did anybody get hurt?" Yolanda asked.

"I'm not going to answer that because I don't know. People can get hurt in many ways. Sometimes a physical hurt is not really a hurt; it's really a matter of perspective."

"Do you believe in God, Dante?"

At first Dante stared at her, surprised at the suddenness of the question. "Yes, but I believe he needs our assistance. I believe God works through us and some people are a little bit better at being a tool than others."

"Are you a good tool?"

"As I said before, I'm deadlier than I look. Now, be nice, and let's talk about something else like Italy's soccer team this year." As they spoke the wind whipped about them and they were jolted by some of the ruts in the road. Yolanda knew she had only a minute or two before they arrived home. "I'll talk about Palermo winning over Milano if you answer one question straight forward."

"Go ahead."

"Remember honestly." She gave him a squeeze.

"I said go ahead."

"How do you make money? You never go to a job, but you always have cash."

Dante pulled over to the curb, near his father's grocery. "See that store?"

"Yes."

"My father is paying me right now so when he passes away every bit of that will go to Marcello. Do you understand? Everything goes to Marcello. And now Yolanda, I'm going to risk everything. Please get off the bike." Yolanda did, thinking she was going to have to walk home. Dante opened his saddle bag. In it were a strange set of tools. "I use these to earn my money."

"What are they? Do you work on cars?"

"I work on locks."

"You're a locksmith?"

"I'm a thief. I really do take from the rich and I really do give, when I can, to the needy. I'm not noble. I just think that someone in a company who makes six-hundred times the lowest paid worker is an asshole. Something is wrong.

You asked for honesty and now you have it." They stared at each other.

"Dante take me home right now."

"Are you angry with me?"

"Yes. Yes. Yes. Yes. I am very...Oh...Dante...I...Oh...It's just not...take me home." She looked intently at him. "Oh you are so very smooth. I should have realized."

"Get on. I'm taking you home right now. Damn it, I could have lied but no, I had to be honest. Why? Because I love her and I can't stop loving her. Get on. Well, yes, Yolanda, I am a thief and a really good one. I only ask you to keep it quiet. Can I trust you for that? Just keep it quiet. If it gets out, everything is ruined. Come on, get on, I'm ready."

"Oh, why shouldn't I be angry? Where else have you stolen and lied? How can I trust a thief? Maybe you'll sneak into my mom's house and take... take... I don't know what you'll take."

"Yolanda, what in the hell would I steal from your mother? I'm after artwork, jewelry, collectibles and things that can be pawned off for ready cash with no questions. In five years no one has been hurt except financially and believe me, Yolanda, it is all covered by insurance. Do you really feel sorry for the people who have the largest, best building in town by lying far more that I do? I can't believe that."

"It's just wrong to steal."

"You stole my heart; is that wrong?"

"There you go, being smooth. Or is it only an act? I don't know what to believe." She turned away. "I'll walk home and... and... don't help on the church, no thieves allowed."

"No thieves in the church? What about Matthew the tax collector or the one next to Jesus at the end? He was one of the very few who recognized him as the son of God. Go ahead walk home, but I'm telling you I have a right to work on that church."

Yolanda turned to face him. "Oh, Oh, what if I told Mama about everything? She wouldn't let you help."

Dante got on the Vespa and stared at Yolanda "That you would never do. Never, because you know that this thief loves you and loves you deeply." And when the Vespa had slowly disappeared into a moonless night, it was dark except for the stars and she was alone.

Chapter 32

Periodically a great deal of mending had to be done. Mama gathered the girls into the room vacated by the Salutatis and gathered every textile in need of repair. Samuel was allowed to romp in the pile of cloth as a small canteen of pizzelles, lemonade and ravioli was set up on the side buffet. There would be no reason to leave the room except to use the toilet and that was down the hall. They played some music, opened the windows and they worked. As they worked they chatted and it was this chatting that was the support of a close family.

It was during this chatting that Rosalina discovered that Yolanda and Dante had had a big fight and that Dante might not be around for awhile. She also found out that Maria's friend, who she had not seen, didn't like hanging around families and from the tone in Maria's voice, Rosalina suspected that perhaps Maria was experimenting with affections. Having trimmed down several sizes, Maria was replacing her joy of eating with other joys and

Rosalina was trying to find another outlet for her daughter's frustrations.

"Tell me, Maria, if you had all the money in the world, how would you live?" Rosalina kept mending not looking at Maria.

"I'd have my own kitchen," said Josephine.

"I'd have my own zoo," said Francesca throwing a ball to Samuel who was learning to throw it back.

"First of all," Maria said, "I'd have an operation so that I could eat anything I wanted and not get fat."

"Not bad," said Rosalina, "but then what?"

"I'd have a large house with a pool and a greenhouse so I could have flowers all year round." Maria stopped mending to think.

"Would you work in the greenhouse or with all that money, have people do the work?" Rosalina looked up.

"No, I'd like to do the work." Maria stopped a moment to think about what she had just said. There was a squeal from Sam as Francesca held the ball listening to the conversation. Maria paid no mind to the noise. "I'd like people to come and see my flowers. That would be very nice." She went back to her job as Mama made a note to ask Sal how difficult it would be to make a small greenhouse just for Maria.

In the garage, which was looking each day a little less like a garage and more like a church, a bathroom had been roughed in and the wiring was nearing completion.

'Where's Dante?' thought Sal. Antonio was crabbing and Roberto was helping Paolo, but he needed someone to help with the pipes and boards. He sat back sweating. "Paolo, I could use another pair of hands. You know anyone who knows something about construction?"

Paolo kept working pulling a line to a junction box as he thought. "Actually I do. His name is Rinaldo. Rinaldo Santucci. He loves working in stone. In many ways that boy is an artist and he loves to sing. If I get him to work here, he will sing all day long, but he's reasonable for the work he does."

"How reasonable? I'm desperate for help," Sal said, hauling some wood to the bathroom.

"You can afford him. Want me to ask?"

"Just bring him with you tomorrow. We'll talk. I'll never get this done on my own and I'd like to put a shower in our own yard like yours. That was a good idea. On a hot day they can run through it to cool off. I'd use it myself."

"You'll need his help with the inside walls and drop ceiling, especially running the juice for the lights. I won't be here at the end of the week because I have a job to do for Mr. Smithington. He wants lights on his new driveway and wall."

Sal perked up. "How do you like the work on that wall? Could Rinaldo do as well?"

"The guy doing it knows his stuff. He allowed space for the wires and he knows how to square. I'd say he was right there with Rinaldo. Do you know the mason? I'm sure Rinaldo would like to meet him."

"He will. It's me." Sal sat back with a grin.

"You?" That stopped Paolo from working. He laughed. "It seems you and I have the same employer." Roberto listened to the two men laugh. He quickly took some photos before the moment was lost as were so many moments in people's lives. They took time to drink some lemonade.

Chapter 33

Dante did not show up and not because of his argument with Yolanda. He had two appointments with two very different people. His first was to see Dr. Frederico Giambattisto at the Alberghetti Institute in Baltimore. The Alberghetti was a museum devoted to all things Italian, particularly in Baltimore, then the east coast then America. After showing the doctor the canvas, Giambattisto told Dante he had a good eye for the pricey archeological find. While the museum evaluated the authenticity of the piece the doctor took a guess and said it was a piece of operatic scenery. Dante went next to his second appointment. Mr. Massimo Salutati. Dante was going to collect on a favor.

With a little homework, Dante had discovered that the property next to the Raphaeli's was owned by a George Matling. He lived in the city and cared nothing for the property, except as a tax write off, and maybe for a future sale. Several people had wanted to buy it but the price was too steep and Matling enjoyed being sought after for the property. It was not a question of profit or even sentiment, it was a question of a deficient personality, but there were many who could fit that description.

"Boungiorno, Massimo," Dante said to a seated figure as he slipped from behind a curtain.

Massimo jumped back, "What? Oh it's you, Dante."

"I haven't seen you around lately, Massimo. You must be busy."

"I...Yes I've been very busy with the new corporation."

Dante moved to a leather chair and sat. "I see you're doing very well."

Massimo looked up at the locked doors wondering how Dante had gotten in. "Yes. Thanks in large measure to you. I owe you a lot."

"I know. That's why I'm here."

"Your not going to tell me what you did to Bono and Moto, are you? Their kids got less than they thought in the will." Massimo wondered if he should have brought up such a sensitive topic.

"I don't think you really want to know."

"I...I...suppose not." He looked down at his desk then up to Dante. "Try to make your request legal, okay?"

"It's not only legal, Massimo, but it's good. It just needs you to make it happen. I want you to find out about a person named George Matling. If he has debts, let me know. I want you to collect all of his I.O.U.'s"

"Then what?"

"Demand instant payment."

"And if he can't pay?" Massimo stared at Dante dreading what he was about to say.

"Tell him you'll take the property next to the Raphaeli's as payment. I know they'll need it sometime, maybe for the kids. Maybe they can build next door. Who knows? Maybe they will even borrow some money from you. One can never tell how the dice will roll." Massimo cheered up, straightened up and smiled. "For the Raphaeli's it will be a pleasure. I can let you know everything in about an hour. Sooner if Puzzi is at home." Massimo picked up the phone. "You can wait here or get a coffee at my son's restaurant next door. Tell Dominic it's on me."

"I know Dominic. He served us dinner when you were ill or something."

"I didn't want to meet you. I was afraid of what you would ask me to do for the favors you did in Sicily. Little did I realize it would be for the Raphaeli's. Now I'm sorry I didn't go." He turned to the phone, "Oh yeah, look, Puzzi, I want you to do something for me."

Dante left to get a coffee. After about an hour having talked to Dominic he convinced him that his place needed some local artwork, and that Yolanda would be a good start. He then returned to Massimo's.

"Find out anything?" Dante asked.

"The guy is nothing but debt. The property is worth about fifty-grand, and his debts are about ten times that. I can pick them up for a song, probably fifteen cents on the dollar or less. I'll have them by tonight. Tomorrow you can hit him with doomsday. How's that for action?"

"How do you explain the loss to your members? Bad investments?" Dante walked back and forth thinking out his plan.

"Never that. The debt will be made up by the deal I made with the city, to finance improvements to the Ballustraud Mansion, and by not charging them for the rent I'm not paying to my son. Now is there anything else I can do?"

"Grazie. No it's enough, Massimo." They shook hands.

"Tell me Dante, do you still carry that stiletto?"

Dante withdrew it and adroitly tossed it to the chair against the wall, its blade striking a shell design at the top. He went over and pulled it out leaving a small indentation. Dante turned to Massimo. "Don't fix it okay? Everytime you see this mark it'll remind you that you're paid up. Now will you please visit the Raphaeli's and their kids?"

"Of course, Signor Dante." He finally smiled, "Tanti Grazie. Arrividerci."

The canvas proved to be part of a 1601 opera scenery done by Augusto Ravelli. It's monetary value was about sixty-thousand to the right buyer, but the museum was not in a position to be that buyer.

"However," said Dr. Giambattisto, "I know someone who can easily afford it and would like to have it, provided you're willing to spend hours negotiating and be willing to take half. His name is Smithington."

"I've heard of him. Do you have an affidavit showing that the piece is authentic and a bona fide estimate as to its likely price."

"That, I can get for you. And I also can set up an appointment with Mr.Smithington." Giambasttisto reached for the phone.

"Don't make the appointment. Just tell him what you have, that it's real, and the price. Let's see what he says. I'll roam around the museum as you talk. I've never seen it.

While Dante was studying some sketches made for Colunna's Hypnopathnia he was approached by a young lady in a museum uniform. "Are you Mr. Dante Bacci?"

"Yes I am."

"Dr. Giambasttisto would like to see you."

Giambattisto was at his desk when Dante walked in. "He's definitely interested. He counter offered ten thousand. We talked and he went to fifteen, then he hung up. Sorry."

"It's better than I thought. Thank you. Is the young lady who brought me here your daughter?"

"My granddaughter. You have a good eye for details."

Chapter 34

It was the habit of Mr.Smithington to retire to his study in the evening with a drink of sherry. He would lock his door and watch a movie. Just as he locked the door a dark figure emerged from the shadows. "Who in the hell are you?"

"Precisely. Now please have a ..." Smithington reached for a button on his desk and it was stopped by a stiletto between his fingers.

Elias Smithington was a man of power and he knew how to get it, use it, abuse it, and he knew when power was being used against him. He sat staring at the figure and waited.

"You have before you on the desk..."Dante retrieved his knife, "a verification of a certain item I would like for you to purchase tonight." Dante conscientiously kept to the shadows.

Elias looked at the affidavit. "It's too much."

"It will go nicely there, where you have a blank wall." The stiletto sped to an empty spot on the far wall.

Smithington jumped from his chair. "My Degas, where is it?"

"Safe for the moment, but..." Dante again retrieved his knife. "Who knows?"

"I don't have fifty thousand on me," Smithington frowned at Dante.

"I think you do, in there." The stiletto once again raced across the room sticking at the edge of a framed Picasso. "I believe that's your safe."

"I could scream for help."

"And by the time they unlocked the door and got in here, I, the Degas and you will be gone. Capice?"

Smithington sat back down. "So if I buy this opera piece of yours, I also get my Degas?"

"Among other things. I'm here to deal, not steal." Dante walked over and got his knife and carefully removed the Picasso from the wall, revealing a safe.

"Thirty-thousand," bargained Smithington.

"Scusi, non capisco. For that amount you get half the Degas. Look at the price on the paper. Sixty thousand. I'm asking fifty thousand. Now who is the thief?" Dante motioned for Smithington to go to the safe.

"How about a check?" Smithington came close to Dante.

"Nice try," Dante said, carefully blocking his face with his gloved hand.

"How do I know I'll get the piece? You could take my money and leave." Smithington put his hand on the knob of the safe .

Dante pointed to a chair that held the opera piece. It had been overlooked by an excited Smithington. "Oh... I...I...see." Smithington managed a brief smile. "And my Degas?"

Dante opened his hand as if to receive cash. "Believe me when I tell you, I'm more dangerous than I look."

The safe was opened and in it were thirty stacks of five-thousand dollars each. Dante opened his sack "Just ten. That was the agreement." Smithington dropped in the money.

"What about the rest of the stuff in there?" Smithington said gruffly. Dante looked at the jewelry and the cash estimating several hundred thousand. "Any more is theft." He moved cat-like across the room.

"And my Degas?" Smithington called out.

Dante pointed to a curtain behind the man. "It's there hiding." By the time Smithington retrieved the painting and made sure it was in good shape, Dante had disappeared.

The next day George Matling was presented with a fait accompli. Pay now or go to court where all of his dealings would be revealed. There would be bankruptcy and disgrace. He pleaded for leniency and Dante presented him with a choice of debt erasure for a small property that Matling hardly cared about. The deal was quickly made and Dante held the deed in his pocket as he drove back to his apartment in his Vespa. Tomorrow he would visit Yolanda to see if she had calmed down.

Chapter 35

With the help of Rinaldo the work on the church progressed rapidly. Singing would suddenly fill the air as Rinaldo sang arias or popular Italian music. Yolanda and her mother kept the men supplied with drink and food as they also painted and promoted the church. Antonio was now fully employed as a crabber since this proved to be a bumper year and Roberto and Dante worked on the photography project. Yolanda made a point of ignoring Dante when he came, making sure she was close to Rinaldo. There were several attempts by Dante to talk to Yolanda to tell her what he had done, but she said, basically, to go away. She was now with Rinaldo who sang, and was very open and honest about life and to Dante, Yolanda looked contented.

By the first of September when everyone was getting ready to go back to school, Mama decided to open the church. Sal and Paolo had finished their jobs for Mr. Smithington who was now installing bars on his windows for some reason. In those last warm days in August when

Paolo stayed many times to have supper, Rosalina would spend time with him walking. One day after dinner they crossed the line seldom crossed on the property and Rosalina showed him where Theresa and Giorgio were buried. Inside the garage Rinaldo was singing to check out the acoustics. He selected a song from La Boehme called Che Gilida Manina. It was a passionate song of a poet for a poor girl with whom he had fallen in love.

As Rosalina listened to the song she turned to Paolo. "I miss my daughter very much, but I know she is gone."

"And what of Giorgio?" Paolo asked.

"Of course I miss him. We were together for 20 years, but..." Rosalina became silent.

"I can't imagine the death of a child. My children are so dear to me; your loss must be great. I am so very sorry, Rosalina." He held her close and she wept and he held her even closer. It was evening and a breeze from the woods seemed to clean the air as if it were taking a deep breath. "She must have been loved by God very much, Rosalina. He must have wanted her back in a hurry." She looked up at him as he said, "The only thing for us to do now is the best for the rest. I know this, Rosalina, in my own way. Everything has a reason. Something is being worked out down here. Maybe we're not supposed to know everything. Maybe that's why he gave us each other, so as to learn." She continued to look at him. The sky was clear and the large reddish moon was just rising. "I love you, Rosalina. I never thought I'd say that to another woman, but I do love you."

She nodded in agreement. And then to the strands of La Boheme, she allowed him to kiss her. It was something she never thought she'd allow another man to do, but she did. "I love you, Paolo, I love you."

It was there in the garage with the voice of Rinaldo bouncing off the false ceiling that a very sun burnt

Antonio got his idea. Dante also listened to the music, but he was not inside the lighted garage. He was on his Vespa in the driveway when he saw Yolanda give Rinaldo a hug for his performance. He had seen enough. It was dark and he was alone.

On the opening day, the first of September, people gathered parking where they could and bringing some token of thanks to Sister Raphaeli for her efforts. Pastor Mike greeted everyone in a Texas drawl and soon the service began. Things went well until Pastor Mike said the words Holy Ghost. A moan came from the heavens. Everyone, including the pastor, stopped and listened. Nothing. He continued his sermon until once again he said Holy Ghost, and another moan came from above. People looked about nervously. Pastor Mike told the audience that when he said a certain word there was a response from heaven, so he said the word again. This time there was a loud long response. A murmur went through the congregation. Was their pastor actually making contact with the Holy Ghost?

Someone in the audience, a tall black man, said, "You better be careful Pastor Mike. It may not be who you think it is. Could be somebody from the enemy camp tryin' to fool us. You be careful."

Mike nodded and softly said, "Holy Ghost."

Between the false ceiling and real one lay a near naked Antonio. He wore only dirty underwear because of the heat and his skin was a dark color. He had placed himself up there as a trick answering to the words Holy Ghost with a moan. He was chuckling to himself at the congregation's response when he saw a large rat making its way toward him. Crabs and eels he could handle, but not rats. He tried to shoo it off, then tried to back away but the congregation's experience was that the spirit on high suddenly emitted an ear piercing scream and a string of expletives. "Get away you filthy thing, get away from me; don't touch me. My God, the rats are coming."

The black man gathered his family around him even as others stood in shock. "I done told you to be careful. Now look what you done did. The devil himself coming down here."

With that Antonio, misjudging the supports, leaned on a ceiling panel which had no support. He plummeted through the ceiling dropping ten feet to the floor of the church.

All that the congregation remembered was a small naked black creature leaping out of the ceiling, falling to the ground, and shrieking about rats.

Calm was finally restored and the service continued but everyone kept their eye on the devil's hole.

Chapter 36

During the first week of September the Raphaelis received visits from Dominic and his parents who brought lots of candies for the kids. The response to these gifts was so gratifying that Mr. Salutati would visit once a month bringing Italian candy. Massimo would be known as the candy man and his fame would last several generations.

Dominic was glad for Rosalina, relieved in many ways of not suddenly becoming a father of eight and Dominic and Paolo got along so well that Dominic as well as his father arranged for some lucrative business for Paolo in their area of the city. In addition to all of this, Dominic displayed nine of Yolanda's paintings of which three sold. Yolanda was surprised about the offer because she did not know that Dante had encouraged Dominic to display her paintings.

At the middle of September Gabe came over the house and informed them that his mother was fine but that Bruno had been put to sleep.

"Sleep?" asked Francesca.

"You mean he never slept?" asked Rolando.

Gabe hesitated, "He's not going to wake up."

"He's dead," said Rolando. "Right? How did it happen?"

"My parents did it. Something was wrong with Bruno, he bit my father and even came after me. My dad was fearful for my mom."

"So he killed him," Francesca said. "Why does it always end that way?"

"Sometimes there is no other choice," said Gabe.

"Can we meet near the spring again?" Francesca asked.

"My father says I can come here. He heard about the church so he wants me to come. Is that okay?"

"Is he going to come to church?" Rolando asked.

"My father says it's difficult to understand the words but he may come if I translate. He wants to show his gratitude to God for helping my mom."

That afternoon it was a house full of children. They were all back in school so an afternoon together was perfect. Rinaldo came over as much as he could but his company had received a large order and he was exhausted at the end of the day which was fine with Yolanda because her senior year was proving difficult.

On September twenty-second they received a call from Cefalu. The person in Italy asked for Salvatore Pasquali and when Sal got on the phone he was informed that his father had had a heart attack. "This is Dottore Minueto. Your mother is very upset and asked me to call." His accent was heavily Sicilian and he struggled to use English until Sal told him to speak Italian. The doctor said that Signor Pasquali was in very bad condition and that Salvatore should come as soon as possible. The doctor then put Sal's mother on the phone.

"This is Salvatore, yes?" She asked.

"Si, Mama, ecco, Salvatore. I'll be there as soon as I can. Listen to the doctor. Everything is going to be fine. Just relax. Okay? Va bene?"

"I am so scared. Come home now, Salvatore. I want my son and my daughter to be here." She spoke in spurts trying to catch her breath.

"Va bene. Relax. I'm coming." Sal shook his head wondering how he could leave quickly.

"When?" came the plea.

"Maybe in three or four days. I'll pay whatever it takes. I'll be there. I'll cancel everything. Don't worry, Mama." Sal was beginning to tear up as he looked at his sister. The kids instinctively gathered because someone dear to them was hurt and they wanted to help.

His mother continued. "Sal, what do you want to eat? I can fix your favorite Friuti di Mare with a garlic sauce and..."

"Mama, please, this is no time to worry about food. Do you mean with the large fava beans from Sardinia?"

"Si."

"Okay, make that. I'll be there." He hung up the phone and told Rosalina .

"Who will take care of the children, the church, or all the work that...?" Rosalina stood in horror at the implications of a journey.

"Rosalina," Sal spoke calmly though his heart was racing, "You have to stay here. I'll go. You will stay here. Everyone needs you here. If it really gets bad, we'll find a way to get you. We'll worry then. Right now I have to get tickets. How in the hell am I going to get tickets to Sicily in three days?"

"Dante," Yolanda said. "He knows how to get anything. Call him."

"Me?" asked Sal. "What about you?"

"We're not talking," Yolanda said in a soft voice.

"You're not talking but as soon as I need something the first words out of your mouth is Dante. Okay, I'll call but...never mind. That's a problem you have to solve."

When Sal called, Dante answered softly as if not knowing who it would be. Sal told him of the problem. "I know it's short notice but..."

"How soon do you need these tickets?"

"In three days. Too soon, eh?" Sal realized this was foolish.

"Why so long? I thought your father was very sick."

"How soon can you get them?"

"What time is it?"

"About ten, why?"

"Can you leave by three?"

"Today?"

"I'll meet you at...just a moment I need to make a call. I'll call you back in less than fifteen minutes. Wait for my call." He hung up. They all waited by the phone silently for twelve minutes until it rang.

"Dante here. There is a flight for Naples at four and a connection to Palermo this evening. From there a train to Cefalu should get us there late tonight. That is where your parents are, correct?"

"Si, si. Tonight? Si. Grazie." Sal was stumbling over his words, reeling with the astounding speed of events.

"I'll pick you up at two. That's four hours. Be ready. Understand? Have your passport and clothes and a little money." Dante was rattling off his own agenda as well.

"What of food?" Sal asked realizing how stupid a question it was.

"Whatever, but you will be rushing about. Be gentle on yourself. How is Mama? I'm sure she wants to go too. And how is Yolanda?"

"Mama is very worried, but fine and Yolanda said she's not talking to you." Sal looked askance at his niece.

"I know. Tell her everything is fine. Right now I have to make a lot of arrangements. Two." He hung up.

Sal just stared at the phone not believing what happened then hung up. "I'll have to ask him how he got tickets so fast."

"Uncle Sal," Yolanda said. "I found out that's not a question to ask Dante."

Dante arrived at two precisely, greeted everyone in a calm but hurried way, and told Mama everything would be fine. He looked around him. "Why are the kids not in school?"

Antonio answered. "It's another teacher's meeting. They're always having teachers' meetings."

"And what about you?" Dante addressed Yolanda.

"The same," she said bluntly as she moved closer to Rinaldo. "And what about you? Stealing a little time for yourself?"

Dante raised his eyebrow at that comment. "I can afford some vacation. All my projects are done."

"Vacation?" Sal turned to him. "Are you going too?"

"Of course. I'm the one with the tickets. You are my guest. Besides, I have a few gifts to buy for my friends. They have done a lot of favors for me."

As the last of the luggage was put in the car, Sal asked Dante, "How much is this costing me? What do I owe you?"

"You wouldn't believe it if I told you." He turned to look at Yolanda with eyes of soft desire. "I only wish you were going."

"Take care of Uncle Sal," Yolanda said.

"Like he was my own uncle. Avanti." They rode off and Yolanda stared in that direction a long time after the car disappeared.

Chapter 37

With all the connections, exchanges and time zones, the two travelers arrived in Cefalu at nine in the morning. Sal walked about as in a dream listening to Dante's commands as the younger man procured a car to drive to the Pasquali's at the western edge of the city toward the hills. The area was strewn with papers and posters hung half glued to walls. The farm was on a gentle rise from which one could see the distant Mediterranean. Oranges were growing as were grapes, figs, tomatoes, and a host of squash type vegetables, but the house showed signs of wear and lack of repair. The owners were poor and elderly.

Sal knocked at the door he had known since youth and was greeted by his mother who appeared to be ready to leave. She stared at him a moment to focus. "Sal, you're here. Bienvenuti, mio caro." She gave him a hug then said, "They took him to the hospital. I didn't know you were coming today so I didn't have time to make you a meal. Are you hungry?" Before Sal could answer she looked over toward Dante. "Who is this young man, the taxi driver?"

Again, before Sal could respond she waved at Dante. "Come, take my bags. I need to get to the hospital." Again she looked at her son. "I'm so glad you have come, now, let's go. Your father is very ill. This may be the last time you see him alive. Come." She walked past the two toward the car. "Well? The bags?" She then gave a smile at Dante who was already picking them up. They made sure she was comfortable in the front seat, Dante acting the role he was assigned with perfection. Why cause questions now? Once they began driving she turned to Sal in the back. "Where did you find such a nice boy? Most of the men around here are crude."

"This, Mama, is Dante. He is a friend of..." Sal began.

"Dante?" Mama interrupted. "I know that name. I've heard it someplace before. Are you from around here?"

"Nice to meet you, Mrs. Pasquali. I hope your husband gets better." Dante decided he'll tell her later when she was more focused.

Enzo was in his own room attended by several nurses and machines constantly recording his status. Sal and his mother talked while Dante sat back and waited. The doctor, a young lady from Messina, told them that Enzo's condition was delicate at best and that he could have another attack at any moment. Dante could read in her eyes that it was all over.

Enzo spoke in lapses. "It was a hard...life. I'm glad you are...in America. I am concerned for...your mother. Take her to...America. Don't let her die...alone. Promise. Please." His eyes saddened and tears started to flow down sun darkened skin wrinkled by years of labor in the relentless sun of Sicily.

"Of course, Papa, whatever you want. You got it. Just rest now. Everything will be done." His father's shoulders sagged as he allowed his full weight to rest. Everyone sat silently in the sleeping man's room. From the window one could see that the harbor was busy with tourists and fishing boats. Dante loved the red tile stucco buildings of Cefalu and the small palm trees that spoke of warmth. Behind the town was a large mountain known simply as "The Rock' and climbing it was an activity of the healthy. Dante watched a small cloud skim by and briefly bring a shadow to the room.

A deep croaking noise brought everyone's attention to Enzo. Machines sprang to life to warn with sounds and lights that the man they monitored was dying. Dante, cat-like, leapt into action, leaving the room to fetch a nurse. Within a minute two nurses followed by the doctor ran into the room, telling everyone to leave. They sat in dreaded silence in a small room with a coffee machine. When the doctor finally arrived she didn't need to say a word. Everyone knew.

"So, it's over," Mrs. Pasquali said, her eyes looking at the wedding ring on her finger. I knew that man for fifty-four years. A lot of struggle, but we raised two healthy children and have a lot of grandchildren, who I never met." She looked up to Sal. "How is Rosalina? I'm sorry she didn't make it. How are her children?"

Sal was too emotional to speak. Dante said, "They are fine, Mrs. Pasquali. Is there anything I can get for you?

No one spoke. "Sal, I want to go home. I want to fix you some spaghetti. You must be..."

"Mama, not now I ..." Sal was wiping tears from his eyes remembering the man who had given him life. The man who had taught him the important things of life. The man who had protected him, fed him, and cared for him. The man he had called father all his life. The man who now lay still in a bed from which he would never rise. A voice he would never hear again.

"Thank you, Mrs. Pasquali," Dante said. "I'm very hungry and spaghetti is perfect." Dante knew she was in shock and doing something familiar was good therapy. It was a safe routine. When he got upset he would shave even if he didn't need one. It was safe. It brought the mind into focus.

Sal nodded almost reading Dante's thoughts. As Sal took his mother to the car, Dante stayed behind to thank people for their efforts and asked what needed to be done. He received some brief instructions then caught up with Sal and his mother just as they reached the car.

At dinner, Mrs. Pasquali set a place not only for the nice taxi driver and Sal but for her husband. "Where is Enzo? He's always in the garden working." She looked outside then came back to sit. She looked across to the empty chair across from her. "If he doesn't come soon, it will be cold. Sal, go get your dad. Is he still in the bathroom?" She turned to Dante. "Do you know where my husband is, young man?"

Sal was staring at his mom when Dante answered. "I believe he is now having dinner with his father."

She looked again across the table where her husband had sat for over half a century. "Si." She slowly lowered her head to the table, Sal moved her plate, and she cried. The two men looked at each other in silence listening to the sound that had reverberated through the ages. It was the sound of loss and grief. It was the sound of the human condition.

Sal escorted his mom to the bedroom after giving her some pain relief medicine then came out to find Dante nibbling at the seafood meal. "This is fantastic, but of course I'm famished. Too much flying."

Sal sat and thought. "I can't eat, now."

"Take my advice, try. Even if you throw up, try."

"She can't stay here. I promised I'd take her to America. She wants to go. How can I afford it?" Sal picked up some pasta with his fork and nibbled.

"What about selling the place?" Dante reached over for some red wine on the shelf. It had a soft brown label declaring it was Chianti. Is this local?"

"It's ours. What a crappy label but it draws your attention." Sal stared at the bottle that brought back memories of his dad's first attempt at bottling and all the problems with the law that made the wine taste even better. "This place has good soil." Again he stopped and thought.

"What's on your mind?" Dante took another sip.

"Sicily has seen many wars. Maybe the red of the wine is more than grapes, eh?" Sal then stood and went to the window looking east. The silence of the room was mildly disturbed by the snoring in the next room. "Do you know just east of us is a volcano?"

"Etna, right?" Dante joined him at the window.

"That thing makes earthquakes." Sal kept staring. "And when the earth shakes, people die, just like in a war. Innocent..." He stopped, walked over and poured a glass of wine and took a deep swallow. "I ...I..."

"Feel free not to talk, but I think it's good if you did." Dante sat back at the table looking around a room that was over three hundred years old. He noticed for the first time that Sal's jacket didn't seem to fit. As a matter of fact it was so far out of style as to be camp.

"I had a wife and two children like I had a father." He nodded to himself. "Fate, eh? A little work, and fate." He looked at Dante. "Single, right?"

"So far."

"Are you sure you want to get involved? There's a lot of sorrow in having close relations."

"It's a choice, isn't it? Even our sufferings are a choice. Happiness is a choice and because of that, I'm willing to take a risk. Perhaps there will be pain but we can learn in that pain. We can give that pain meaning."

Sal smiled. "I had this conversation recently with a bunch of kids. Thank you for reminding the teacher of his own lesson."

Dante sipped more wine. "Sal, I need to ask. Where in the blazes did you get that jacket?"

Sal looked down. "I don't know. It was in a pile of clothes next to Roberto's camera. I was in a hurry."

Dante only shook his head. "You were about to say something about selling the house."

"This house goes back a long way. It's seen a lot of history. It'll be tough but if it means selling to get Mama to America and set up to be near us and her near the grandkids, then I'll sell. In many ways it might be good to cut all the ties." Sal poured a small amount of wine. "Be careful, Dante. It's warm out and this can pack a punch."

"What would be the best for everyone, Sal? Living with you?" Dante put down his glass.

"Ideally she'd live very close but not with us. I could get a trailer and put it on the property, but there goes the privacy and some plans I had, but..." he shrugged.

"What would it cost to build a small house for her if you already had the property like next door?" Dante was broaching the topic as gently as he could.

"Matling? That son of a bitch wouldn't sell that piece of land, especially if he knew I wanted it. Way too much." Sal put his glass down. "You mean if I already had it? Oh, I could get a nice place with some sweat equity for under forty grand, but when did we start dreaming? When did we start dreaming?"

"Then don't sell this house, exchange it." Dante got a glass of water and drank it. "This water is fabulous. Maybe that's the stuff in the wine."

"Exchange? With who?"

"Me" Dante reached into his pocket and pulled out some folded papers and an envelope. "Here is the deed to Matling's property. All you have to do is sign it and it's yours." He placed it in front of a shocked Sal who only stared at it. "And here in this envelope is a cashier's check for fifty grand. We both need to sign that. What I want is the deed to this property." He placed the check in front of Sal who looked at it then at Dante.

Instinctively Sal reached into his jacket for a pen and found a card instead. He looked at it. It was proof of membership in the Italian Fascist Party. He placed it on the table looking up at Dante. "What the hell is going on? What you're giving me is ten times the worth of this house and I could go to jail. I know I'm in shock. Tell me all this is true."

Even as he denied what was happening Sal thought of the greenhouse for Maria, the petting zoo for Francesca and Rolando, more fig trees, and a dam to block off the stream that belonged to him for a swimming hole.

Dante poured a small amount of water in his glass and with a flick tossed it at Sal's face. The water sprayed off his face and down his front. Sal took the pen from Dante's hand, signed the papers, then took a deep breath. "Thanks." He did not wipe off any of the water. "But why?"

"Let's say I fell in love with Sicily."

"Let's say you fell in love with a Sicilian, eh?"

Chapter 38

"Sal, I don't want Yolanda to know about this deal right now. I want her to want me like I want her, not as an obligation for something I did. If she decides she doesn't want me then let it be fate. You see she thinks I'm a thief and wants nothing to do with me." Dante looked again around the ancient room he had just bought.

"Are you a thief? How did you get those tickets so quickly? I was told not to ask questions like that of you. Is she right?"

"It wasn't easy, Sal. Just like it wasn't easy to get that property."

Sal looked down at the table wondering if he was doing the right thing. "Is everything legal what we're doing? Please tell me yes, otherwise all the deals are off. I don't think you're a thief, just a grand manipulator. A bender of laws, right?"

"Everything we are doing is legal. There is some stretching but the law needs some exercise. You could ask me how I can go to Italy whenever I want or do expensive shopping in Naples when I don't have a job. All good questions. Well, I make deals that carry a certain element of fear on the other person's part and a risk on my part. I made a deal one night with a certain Grande Signore for whom you built a wall."

"Smithington. Now there's a criminal."

"And in the process of making that deal he, in his excitement, made a simple mistake of putting in my sack too much money. I saw what he did, but kept quiet. Am I a thief for not saying something to a man who willingly gave me too much? Some would say yes; others would wonder why I would bring up the question." Dante moved slowly about the room. A warm breeze came through the open window. He could feel evening. "Sal, I may be considered dishonest, but there is one thing where I am very honest. I love Yolanda. I fell in love with her one evening on a bocce court. She was about to kiss Marcello and I interrupted them. I knew then I wanted Yolanda as my wife. I will not lie or cheat to get that love. It must come on its own." He was about to say more but thought of the good taste of the wine. "You know with a little promotion and marketing that wine could prove a gold mine."

The arrangements were complex but Dante stayed with the Pasqualis until they were on their way to America from Naples. Mama Pasquali was sad but resigned to her husband's death. She had learned to survive earthquake, war, poverty, disease, and bad government. And now the loss of a husband. She told Sal that she really did not want to stay in the house and looked forward to America. Even at her age, she thought of it as an adventure. An adventure from which she would not return. When Sal told her about building a church she brightened even more. "Enzo wouldn't like it but the grandchildren would. I'm for it."

Dante stayed in Naples a few days doing some shopping then on an urge he wanted to return to Cefalu. He wanted to become acquainted with the place, and the neighbors He wanted to take off half a year to be there at harvest, to do some repairing, and to become Sicilian.

The stone house with its red tile roof was over three hundred years old. There was a basement with a spring, two levels and several sheds. From the top floor that had a small balcony, he could see the Mediterranean. The sheds contained tools, bottles, a bag of cork, a potter's wheel, and a Gerry-rigged kiln. There were also shelves for drying vegetables and a forno that appeared not to have been used in years. Dante decided to take time to do some drawing not only of the house but of the surrounding countryside and the people.

One day Dante was mending the east wall that supported the fava beans when he saw a person coming up to him. He was an old man of perhaps seventy. He moved slowly hoisting his baggy pants occasionally and even in the heat he wore a thin sweater. "Boungiorno," he said. Dante liked the sound of Sicilian Italian.

"Como sta?" Dante returned the greeting.

The man looked at Dante's work. "You need help?"

"I always need help. What can you do?" Dante spoke in Sicilian.

"What you're doing, only I do it right. When the beans get heavy, they'll pull what you did from the wall. Then the beans won't be worth the fart." He smiled showing many teeth missing. One of the costs of poverty.

"Okay. Show me what you can do. I'm going to fix the forno so that I can bake bread." Dante started to hand the man his gloves, but he pulled his own out from his back pocket. Dante nodded and went to the forno.

"It only needs to be clean. It's in good shape," the man called after Dante.

"How do you know that?" Dante stopped, amazed.

"Because I built it before the war and it never had a problem. Enzo got lazy so he started to buy his bread." The man evaluated the string shaking his head. "Needs wire and stucco nails. I know where they are."

"You built this before what war?"

"Mussolini's war." He walked to the shed with the tools.

The man not only was older than he looked, but healthier, and familiar with the house. "My name is Dante," Dante approached him.

"Agostino." They shook hands. "I use to help Enzo, but he got weak. I told him to eat more garlic, but he didn't listen. He looked at Dante. "I've heard your name before."

"What did Enzo pay? I hope I can be as generous," Dante asked.

"Enzo paid what he could. I'm happy to work. He let me stay in the big shed, the one with the potter's wheel. Upstairs. Deal?" he stood patiently waiting for Dante to decide his future.

"Sure, why not? Don't you have a family?" Dante wasn't sure about getting involved.

Agostino smiled. "I'm a poet. My family has gone to other places or died. I could have gone but here is my home among the ancient gods." He smiled again. "No, I'm not crazy. One day you'll understand if you stay. In those hills and in those woods and rivers, the old gods are very much alive, but right now I have to put up some bean strings and help my new master with an oven." He started to leave but stopped and turned to face Dante, "Bienvenuti, Signor Dante. Here is where your real life begins and it may not be what you think."

Chapter 39

The news of Enzo's death sent a shock through the Raphaeli household. The children had never met him but his name had been spoken with such reverence that it was as if an icon had fallen. When Sal returned home with his mother, another shock went through the family. Mrs. Pasquali was introduced to the children as Nonni and each of them wanted to tell her everything they were doing bringing out cameras, crab nets, stuffed animals, jewelry, and paintings. Nonni was overwhelmed and asked only to rest.

"Can't you see," said Mama, "That she is an old woman and has come thousands of miles to be here? I'll call you one at a time and each of you can meet her and tell her about what you're doing and for God's sake don't ask her about her family or husband. Right now I have to talk to Uncle Sal about what happened. So, go. Do something useful."

Sal realized that what he had to say would be complex. "Mr. Matling sold his property to us, Rosalina."

"You had to go to Italy for that?"

"No, Dante made some arrangements so that we could do some exchanging for the land. He also got some money for us to build a small house for Mama so that she could live next to us. That way the children can see her anytime and she can see us. Isn't that very good? She said she even wants to be a part of the church." Sal felt good that he got all of that out in one breath.

Rosalina listened then hesitated. "Matling sold the property to us? Why would he do that?"

"Maybe he didn't like our church or maybe he didn't like the noise, who knows?" Sal swallowed realizing it sounded thin. "I'm only sorry that Papa didn't make it." He was hoping for a change in the topic.

"Sal," Rosalina said. "Something is going on. Papa wanted to die in Sicily. Only Mama wanted to come here. Tell me about the house?"

Sal took a deep breath. "I exchanged it for the Matling property and some money so that Mama could live with us. It was a good deal, don't you think?"

"Exchanged? You didn't buy it? Who made the arrangements? Does Matling now own our house in Sicily? Why would that old fart want to live in Italy? He can't speak English let alone Italian. Sal, what the hell is going on? Do we still have the house in Sicily? Who owns it?" Rosalina had stood and was pacing as she ranted.

"Was Dante there, Uncle Sal?" asked Yolanda who had come in with Rinaldo.

Sal glanced up. "Of course." Sal did not want to discuss Dante.

"Where is he now?" Yolanda asked. Rosalina stared at her.

"He stayed in Italy to do some shopping. He had gifts to buy for..."

"Did Dante have anything to do with these arrangements?" Yolanda stepped away from Rinaldo with a stern expression.

"He had a great deal to do with the arrangements." Sal glanced at his sister who had now concentrated on her brother.

"Including the money and the house for grandmother?"

"Yes." Sal slowly stood and became serious. "Listen to me, Yolanda. What I am about to tell you I promised not to say but it needs to be said." He looked in the direction of Rinaldo. "Dante loves you very much. Everything he has done he has done for you and for the good of the family. He has done nothing for himself." He stood staring at them.

"And he's in Italy now shopping?" Yolanda asked.

"Perhaps he went back to Cefalu."

"Why there?" Rosalina asked

"To be in his new home." Sal sat waiting for the attack.

"Do I know this place, Uncle Sal?" asked Yolanda. Tears were forming.

"You've seen pictures of this place, but Yolanda you've never been to Sicily," Sal said.

"Does he like his new home?" Yolanda was stifling her tears. Why had Dante done this? Was it for him? Was it to have Grandma come? What would he gain living there instead of here? Why would he sacrifice so much money for them? Would he sacrifice his own happiness for them? He was there, and she was here and she couldn't see him. Did he stay because she rejected him and he couldn't stand seeing her with another man? What was happening? What did she need to do? Curse him? Thank him? Love him? She was confused. Something needed to be done.

As Yolanda struggled to grasp the events, Sal kept talking. "Right now the harvest is ready. Dante will have his hands full alone. He will need to..."

"Uncle Sal," Yolanda broke into his speech. "I..." She looked at her mother. "Mama...I..." she stopped again then looked at Rinaldo. "Oh, Rinaldo, you are such a good friend but..." She looked at all of them. "I'm very confused."

"Stop right there." Rinaldo grabbed both her arms. "Do you think I'm such a fool that I couldn't see what you two meant to each other. Look, I came here to work on a church and sing and I found a nice Italian girl who made part of my summer pleasant. If you're confused, Yolanda, go get some answers. I'm not going anywhere and if you need help you know where to find me."

She kissed him on the cheek and hurriedly went to her room.

Chapter 40

Dante sat alone on the balcony overlooking the garden. He owned just under three hectares and it needed repairs. He wondered if old Agostino was up to the work. A few neighbors had come over to tell them about a person named Lorenzo who was using his influence with local officials to stop many of the people from selling their food in town or from forming an association to get a better price for export. When Dante asked Agostino about Lorenzo he was told that the man is a bully and full of brag like the Fascist's were. One good push and they fall, but you'd better be good at pushing. Dante just sat and thought watching the evening stars appear as the colors of the day changed to a velvet in a near cloudless sky.

He was planning two visits that evening. The first to some members of the syndicate he had met the last time he was here and who he had helped and who in turn owed him a favor. The other visit would be a late night encounter with Lorenzo himself explaining to him how it would not be to his advantage to trouble the syndicate. With a little persuasion, Lorenzo would allow the corporation to be formed.

He was preparing for his presentation with a few accurate flips of the stiletto when he heard a noise in the other room. He thought it was Agostino coming in for a late snack, but he usually made his presence known by a cough. There was a rustle of curtain in the warm breeze. "Bouno sera. Che es?" There was no answer. He walked into the other room cautiously thinking that perhaps Lorenzo had taken the initiative. As he entered he saw a gossamer figure watching him. "Who are you?"

The phantom answered, "Beatrice, Dante" and stepped into the light. It was Yolanda.

Dante stared in disbelief. "Yolanda. You take my breath away. How did you get here? Perhaps I should ask why you are here? You took a risk at coming. I could have been out or..." He stopped. "Sal told you, didn't he?"

"My brother took a risk to save a bird. Without risk, what is life? Dante why did you buy this house? What are you risking?" She moved toward him.

"I had planned to make a life for myself here, Yolanda. Since I couldn't have you, this place would be the closest I could get to you and I would make it work because it is already a beautiful place and filled with a rich history." He moved toward her. "These people are having trouble with a bully. I want to help them and I will need help. I need help to run this place, but it is a risk because it is poor." Dante thought that here before him was the one woman he most loved. Here before him in an ancient land where the old gods were still alive was a person for whom he would risk everything. Here was the woman who would make life worth living, but would she risk everything?

Yolanda looked out the window to the sea as she placed her hand into his. "Look, Dante, a crescent moon over the water." She then turned to face him. "With love, Dante, there is no risk. There are only the stars that have been with us since the beginning."

Dante liked what he heard, but there was a tremble in her hand.

Chapter 41

Even before Christmas and because of Christmas Yolanda wanted to return home. By November despite the warmth, the harvest, and her affection for Sicily, Yolanda wanted to go home. She missed her family, she missed the familiar landscape and she found it difficult to constantly talk in another language. She had tried, but it just wasn't working. When she told Dante of her struggle, he said that he understood and told her that whatever decision she would make, he supported her. She left on the first of December and that was four years ago.

Dante stayed for about a year writing to Yolanda with increasingly less frequency until one day he wrote a brief but stunning letter stating simply that he had given the farm to St. Leo's church in Cefalu and then there was only silence.

Weeks grew into months and months into years and at first Yolanda was extremely distraught. She was so distraught that she almost did not complete her last year of school, but through the encouragements of her Uncle

Sal and the stern warnings from her Mama she completed high school.

In the middle of all the emotional turmoil Mrs. Pasquali died on the back porch of her new home that faced the greenhouse. Almost at the moment of her death Tino released a long wail that brought Sal's attention to the dog and eventually to where Tino was looking.

At the funeral, which was Catholic and formal, Yolanda was consoled by Rinaldo and soon they were dating. It was also at the funeral that Sal noticed a bearded priest that kept looking at the family. When Sal asked Father Blanco who the priest was, Blanco said it was Father Raymondo from the Annapolis parish. This Raymondo had only recently graduated from the seminary but was already of interest to the bishop. "He has a good mind, Mr. Pasquali, but there is more to being a priest than thinking," Father Blanco said. "And tell me, Sal, how is this church of yours is doing?"

"It's been a struggle because the people are so poor but we get a lot of help. Rosalina loves to play the piano and make meals; Antonio and Roberto sing and come up with all sorts of things to entertain the congregation. They even started a newsletter which Rosalina edits."

"She edits it?" asked the priest.

"Yes, the boys started to put the telephone numbers for girls in the congregation, so ..." Sal shrugged. "You know how that is."

"And what about Yolanda?" the priest asked. "It's been rough on her hasn't it?"

"Oh, she got her grandmother's house and she has Rinaldo but ..." Sal scratched his ear. "I believe she's still in love with Dante."

"And where is he?"

"We don't know." Sal looked around being sure he wouldn't be heard. "I think Yolanda is going to marry Rinaldo." He shook his head.

"And how is your sister Rosalina? Is she getting serious about Mr. Dondi?" The priest looked around to see if Paolo was there. He was; he was at the door and seemed impatient.

Sal smiled. "You may see a double wedding before the end of this year, Father Blanco."

"But not Catholic, right?" Blanco asked.

"No, it will be Pentecostal but you will be invited and I want you to bring Father ..."

"Raymondo. I'll ask but from what I know of him, he is a very private man." He looked around too see if he could find Raymondo. He couldn't. He turned back to Sal "What about Rosalina's kids? I heard Antonio got in trouble with the law."

Sal rolled his eyes. "Yes, but it shook him up. Do you know he now wants to be a lawyer? A lawyer. I can't imagine Antonio being a lawyer."

Rosalina came up. "Sal, we have to leave. I have to ..." She stopped. "Oh, Father Blanco, nice to see you. Please come over for something to eat after the funeral."

"Glad to, Rosalina. How are the kids? Sal was telling me about Yolanda and Antonio."

Rosalina wanted to leave, glancing up at Paolo who was pacing near the door. "Sam started school so I have more time for my church. It's very different than St. Gabriella."

"Only in method, Rosalina, only in method. What is Rolando up to? The last thing I heard he was saving the whales or was it porcupines?"

"Rolando," Rosalina said, "will probably become a Buddhist. He used the word sentient the other day. When I looked it up I discovered anything living is sentient."

Father Raymondo walked past them taking some photos. Sal watched the priest, feeling somehow close to him.

"Sal?" Father Blanco interrupted Sal's thoughts. "What of the twins, Roberto and Maria? They seem so grown up."

Before Sal could answer Rosalina said, "Sal, I'm going home with Paolo. Rinaldo will take Yolanda and I'll take Rolando, Josephine, and Francesca. You can take the rest, okay?" She nodded at the priest then quickly went to Paolo.

Father Blanco followed her with his eyes. "She's still not forgiven God for Theresa, has she? Only when she does, will she be forgiven." Sal said nothing. The priest turned back "And the twins?"

"Well, Roberto wanted to be an architect and Maria is going into cosmetics. She wants her own barber shop. She will be the one to continue what her great grandfather had begun. I can help her with that goal."

"And Josephine? Didn't she like cooking? I heard she was the protégée of...Hmmm... I've forgotten his name, you know the owner of Massimo."

"Dominic," Sal volunteered.

"Yes, of course Dominic. Is she still learning?"

"Yes, and even at fourteen Josephine knows her way around the town." Sal seemed proud of her.

"So the family is growing up." The priest seemed to be ending the conversation.

"You didn't ask about Francesca," Sal said.

"Francesca," the priest repeated. "Of course that was who I forgot. How is she doing?"

"Francesca will be our writer. She will be the one who will be our memory and tell others of what has happened." Sal looked toward the door where Francesca was leaving with her mother.

"Oh, Mr. Pasquali." It was Marcello. "I'm so sorry about your mother. When Pop died last year I thought it was the end of the world. I couldn't do anything. It seems that when someone you love dies, it doesn't seem fair for everything to go on as usual, but it does, doesn't it? It just goes on." He shook hands with Sal then with Father Blanco. "You were there for my father, too. Thank you."

Father Blanco smiled, "That's what priests do."

As Marcello talked to Father Blanco, Sal noticed the bearded priest putting his camera into a saddlebag of a Vespa and drive off.

Within a short time there was a double wedding. Yolanda married Rinaldo and Rosalina married Paolo. Rosalina gained two of Paolo children and Yolanda had one of her own—a baby girl she named Beatrice. Everyone thought she had named it after her grandmother but she confided one day to Uncle Sal as they worked together in a much larger garden that her daughter was named after a woman in a story she had read called, the Divine Comedy."

Chapter 42

The discovery of the real identification of Father Raymondo was made by accident by Rosalina as she was getting information for her monthly church newsletter. She was gathering the names of all the 'people of the cloth' in the area. She wanted to know their background, their education, their interests and their experiences. She was developing a network.

When she received a letter from the Archdiocese concerning Father Raymondo, Rosalina sat in stunned silence. He was none other than Dante Bacci. Not even Marcello knew. Dante had changed his name and had become a priest. From what Rosalina understood he had insisted on being a part of the Annapolis community of St. Anthony. 'Why?' she thought, 'Why wouldn't Dante tell us about what he was doing? Why would he allow Rinaldo to marry Yolanda? He has done so much for us yet he suddenly disappears and reappears as a priest. Why? Should I tell Yolanda? Or Sal? Or Anyone? If he does not want to be known should I betray that?' She folded the letter and put it on the table away from the other letters.

The next day Sal got the mail and noticed two letters for the Santuccis. The mail carrier had given them the wrong letters. Sal put them on Rosalina's table as a reminder to bring them to Yolanda. About midday Sal told his sister about the miss-delivered letters. The letters sat there on the table until Paolo noticed them. When he asked Rosalina about them he was told they belong to Yolanda and Paolo sent Rolando to deliver them.

When Yolanda got the letters she was in the middle of changing Beatrice, so she told her brother to just put them on her desk, and there they sat for several days until late one night when things were quiet Yolanda read the letter from the Archdiocese.

Upon reading of Dante, Yolanda didn't know whether to be happy, sad, angry, curious or all of the above. She felt she had no choice but to visit Father Raymondo.

Without consulting anyone, Yolanda decided to visit Dante telling Rinaldo she just wanted to go window shopping on her own. When she arrived at St. Anthony's which had a view of the harbor she was told that Father Raymondo was working on a mural for the church in the annex.

"A mural?" Yolanda asked.

"Yes," said the deacon, a small framed man of about sixty. "He is very good with his hands. He is a very good painter." There was something effeminate about his composure.

Yolanda was escorted to the annex and the deacon pointed to a figure high on a rickety scaffold. He was painting birds. To the left of the figure was a massive statue of St. Michael, his wings outstretched to protect the ones chosen by God. She noticed in a corner behind a picture was a dark blue Vespa with two saddlebags.

She waited for awhile remembering the work she had done on the garage but this project was twenty times larger. The deacon was about to call but Yolanda shouted, "Dante."

The person stunned by the explosive sound of his real name in a vaulted, serene area, lost his footing and as he turned he faced open space. He awkwardly grabbed at the scaffold releasing the paint in his hand for a firmer grip but his foot slipped. In his initial fall he held to the scaffold hoping against hope that the structure would support him. It didn't. He pulled the scaffold as he fell. At the last moment he found a place to hold on to Michael's wing but the scaffold plummeted to the ground bringing with it paint and brushes.

"As Dante clung to angel's wing he felt the massive support rush past him hitting the marble floor with such a concussion that Yolanda and the deacon braced themselves against the far wall. Dante slowly let himself slide from the wing down the mantle of dress and to the floor.

The deacon immediately ran off to tell the authorities of what had happened not caring for the possibility that a priest could have been killed.

Dante walked toward Yolanda slowly then just stood in front of her. "Hello, Yolanda. That was some entrance."

"Why?" asked Yolanda. "I thought you were dead. I tried very hard to find out..."

"I didn't want you to know," Dante said. They stared at each other.

"Why not?" Yolanda was confused. She glanced around the room, she looked at the mural, at the debris on the floor, at the paint stained marble, then back to Dante.

"Yolanda, I could see what you wanted; your eyes told the entire story. You wanted a family, security, and a safe routine, right?" Dante motioned to the door. Let's take a walk. It's a beautiful night." He paused. "You had a chance to see Sicily, but you decided that it wasn't what you really needed. It was someone else's dream, not yours.

"I...I...loved you very much." Yolanda walked with him to the door."

"And I love you." Dante and Yolanda went outside. They could see in the distance the busy harbor. They could see the people shopping and doing all the domestic things that people do.

"But?" Yolanda asked "There's a huge question there, Dante."

"I love you Yolanda as ..." Dante stopped and looked deeply into here eyes. "Yolanda, I do love you but ..." he stopped. He stared at her lips. He wanted to kiss them. He wanted to make love. "You named your little girl Beatrice. Was it Dante's Beatrice?"

"Of course." She too looked at Dante's lips. She too wanted him.

"It can't be, Yolanda. You're married...and ..."

"For you I would risk, Dante. Really I could ..."

"No." Dante held her hand. "Fate and you have made that decision. There is something being worked out, Yolanda. No matter what your feelings are, you were meant to be with a safe person. You needed someone you could trust and someone who could trust you. Did you tell Rinaldo you were coming to see me?"

Yolanda shook her head, "No. No I didn't. I didn't want to hurt his feelings."

"His feelings? Yolanda you've come to visit a priest."

"You're more than a priest to me, Dante." Yolanda began to well up.

"No, Yolanda, that's where you're wrong, you see that's what I am. I am a priest. You may have feelings for that priest but I am a priest." Dante looked out toward the harbor. "When you left Sicily, there was very little for me.

Had you not come, I would have made a life there, but your rejection forced me to look carefully at what I really wanted. It was then that Agostino invited me to attend Mass at St. Leo's, the very church of the chandelier, so I went. During Mass I realized what was missing in my life. I went to confession and a Father Di Luccia heard me. After that, it was easy to talk to Agostino of my past. He asked me for the stiletto and when I gave it to him he said that the answer to my questions had always been in my hand but that I had been holding it incorrectly. He turned the stiletto around and stuck it into a log. He told me that that was the correct way to see the it. When I looked, I knew what I had to do."

"So you became a priest?" Yolanda asked studying him.

"Yes, Yolanda, I became a priest."

Yolanda turned from him in anger, then turned back, "Tell me, tell me that you don't love me then I'll go away."

Dante hesitated, "I do love you Yolanda. I love you as a child of God. I love you with the fullness of all that is holy between two caring people. I love you as myself and I love with a passion that goes beyond physical ..."

"No, I don't want that. I want you. I want the physical. I want to be held. I want to feel your body next to me. I'm not made to be angelic; I am of this earth, Dante." She stared at him, "If you can't give that kind of love then to me there is no love. I need to be touched, to be kissed, to be...to be..." she stopped. Yolanda was beginning to cry. Dante came toward her. "No, don't touch me, that's my husband's role. I want a love that's jealous; I want a love that belongs only to me. No." She turned and walked away.

Dante stood watching after her until there was nothing to see but the distant harbor lights. He stared, thinking of what she had just said and slowly Dante looked up to the stars. He thought that he was now truly alone but as he looked at the stars he knew that he was not alone. He knew he had never been alone.